MW00896855

Black Tea

By
Madhu S. Madhukar
(2008)

iUniverse, Inc.
New York Bloomington

Black Tea

The story is about India's bias against darker skin color, particularly pertaining to women.

This is a work of fiction. All of the characters, names, incidents, organizations, and dialogue in this novel are either the products of the author's imagination or are used fictitiously.

iUniverse books may be ordered through booksellers or by contacting:
iUniverse
1663 Liberty Drive
Bloomington, IN 47403
www.iuniverse.com
1-800-Authors (1-800-288-4677)

ISBN: 978-0-595-53018-2 (pbk)
ISBN: 978-0-595-63072-1 (ebk)

Printed in the United States of America

iUniverse rev. 12/04/2008

Acknowledgement

I acknowldge many crucial inputs from my 16 year old son, Neel, and 13 year old daughter, Priyam who contributed significantly to make this story more readable. It gives me an immense pleasure to see that now my children are in a position to be my teacher – the roles have been successfully reversed.

CHAPTER I

An Imperfect Family

The monsoon was in full fury and it had been raining the whole day. The potholes in the street were overflowing with water. The two-lane street in front of her office building was packed tight with rows of cars, motorcycles, auto rikshaws, city buses, bicycles, and pedestrians, all trying to beat others to get ahead to reach their destination. The drenching rain compounded the traffic confusion.

Maya moved the curtain to one side and looked outside the window of her 10th floor office window. The traffic on the packed streets was barely inching forward. "How was she going to find a taxi to get home in this rain and traffic?" she wondered. She wanted to go home early today. She had to do something very important for her 22 year old daughter, Natasha. She returned to her desk and looked at the clock on the computer monitor. It was flashing 4:30 pm. She reluctantly decided to work a little longer and wait out the traffic. She picked up a file from a stack of papers on her beautiful mahogany desk, picked up a pencil in her right hand and started reading it.

Being a Senior Manager in a multinational bank, Maya had many responsibilities and often worked late or even after work at home. In spite of her involvement in many high profile projects, she kept her office spic and span and very organized. She had always been a clean freak and always preached her subbordinates that the presentation of a product is as important as the product itself. In spite of the tough standards that she imposed on her subordinates, they loved to work under her leadership. They loved her compassionate side and the fact that she would always go out of her way to help those in need. However, from the last couple of weeks she had been acting different. She would appear a little more testy than normal.

She tried to concentrate on reading the reports, but her mind was somewhere else. She again looked outside the window to assess the weather. Not knowing how to kill the time, her eyes wandred around her office. She gazed at the framed photograph of her family portrait hanging on the wall across her desk. The frame was slightly tilted. Being a perfectionist, she got up immediately and tapped the picture frame slightly from one side until it looked perfect. The picture showed her sitting with her husband, Om, in the middle and her son, Vikram, and daughter standing behind them. By all standards she had a perfect family – a loving husband, a handsome son, and a very beautiful daughter. She stood there staring at the picture. The reflection of frequent lightening off the glass frame would brighten up the picture. The picture stirred mixed emotions in her. While, the prankish look in Vikram's eyes brought smile on her face, looking at Natasha's picture transformed her smile from pure joy to a mixture of joy and worry. "It is my fault," she blamed herself. "She is so beautiful and intelligent," she pondered, "Why did God not give her the thing she needed the most." Her eyes dampened a little. With her index finger she touched the pictures of her children and gently kissed it.

She returned to her desk and tried to kill some more time. She could still hear the thunderous rain. Occasionaly she would look at the computer monitor and then toward the window to see if the rain had eased. The rhythmic sound of pouring rain was suddenly broken by one of her favorite musical ringtones coming from her cellphone. From the ringtone, she knew it was Natasha. She immediately took her phone out of her purse and walked near the window.

"Are you already home?" she asked.

"Yes *Maa*[1], where are you?" asked Natasha.

"The weather is really bad here," she replied while peeking outside the window, "I decided to wait out the rain but it looks like it's not going to work. I am leaving now. I'll try to catch the city bus."

"You take your time *Maa*. I'll get dinner ready meanwhile," said Natasha.

---

1 English translations of non-english words used in this book are given at the end of the book.

"No, don't cook anything new," she instructed, "We have enough leftovers from yesterday."

She decided to brave the weather. She collected her stuff and as soon as she was about to switch the computer off, there was ringing coming from her computer. It was Om calling her on video chat. She answered the ring and Om's picture showed up on the screen.

"Om, it's pouring here and the traffic is backed up. I don't know when I'll reach home," she told her husband.

"The situation is same here at my end too. I've a class in a few minutes. I'll come home as soon as I finish my class," said Om, "Hopefully the weather will improve by then."

"Natasha is already home. I'm leaving now," she said.

"I hope you remember what you have to do tonight," he said, "It's very important that we send Natasha's pictures to Mr. Mathur by tomorrow."

"Yes, I know," she said, "That is why I am anxious to go home while there is still daylight."

"Well, in that case I'll let you go. We'll discuss this more at dinner."

CHAPTER II

A Primer On Color Discrimination

"So…does anybody have any questions?" Professor Om Prakash Srivastava asked.

A very dark skinned girl student, SUNITA, 22, raised her hand.

"Yes Sunita?"

"Compared to our parent's generation, how prevalent is color discrimination now?" asked Sunita.

"Well Sunita, there is no quantitative data to compare between the two generations," Prof. Srivastava pondered, " but I think we can safely say that color sensitivities are on decline. At least people have openly started talking about it now. Although I believe, it'll take several generations before people start to appreciate the beauty of every shade of skin color."

Another very dark skinned male student, SHRIKANT, 21 raised his hand.

"Yes Shrikant?"

"Is the extent of color discrimination the same for males and females?" asked Shrikant.

"That is a very good question. What do you think?" Prof. Srivastava asked back.

"As you can see, Sir, I am quite *kaala*," replied Shrikant with a little grin on his face.

The whole class laughed as Prof. Srivastava smiled.

"My younger sister is also *kaali,* and I think my parents, especially my mother, are a little more concerned about her than they are about me," continued Shrikant.

The class had finally gotten involved in the spirited discussion. Prof. Srivastava walked around the classroom observing how interested his students were.

"Well, how many of you think that color discrimination is gender dependent?" he asked.

Almost every student raised a hand. Prof. Srivastava looked around the class, surprised at unanimity of the class.

"Why do you all think gender plays such a significant role?" he asked.

"I think because girls are considered the weaker part of our society. They are easier targets," responded ANJALI, another 21 year-old girl.

"Good Anjali, but next time please raise your hand. Anybody else?" asked Prof. Srivastava again.

Om looked around the class to spot any raised hands. Seeing no volunteers, he continued, "Well, since all of you have decided you have nothing to say I'll tell you what I think. I concur with you all about your observations that Indian males are not subjected to as rigorous color scrutiny as girls, and this is my take on it."

"At the beginning of civilization it was a survival, and cultural, necessity to produce as many male offsprings as biologically possible. These males would be needed to win battles for their tribes and families, take part in hunting, and provide strength to increase the likelihood of the family survival."

"What do you think the role of women was in these scenarios?" asked Prof. Srivastava after a little pause.

"The role of women was mostly to make babies - preferably male babies," responded one student.

"That is right," said Prof. Srivastava with a laugh, "Although I hate to admit it, girls were needed primarily for their reproductive engines, provide help in "mundane" household chores, and to play supportive roles for physically stronger males."

Another girl, RITA, 20 raised her hand.

"Yes… is it Ritika?"

"Actually sir I go by Rita, and I've a question: why do only girls face color discrimination?" asked Rita.

Prof. Srivastava paused to think.

"I would hypothesize that girls still face color discrimination because some remnants of gender discrimination have survived. The most important of those is that sons are still considered pillars and torchbearers of a family; and thus, just having a son – *gora* or *kaala* – is at least half the answer to parents' prayers," he answerd, "Perhaps this is why Indian parents are generally more forgiving of their son's skin color."

He continued, "But girls, especially dark skinned ones, have to win two battles – number 1- As Anjali said earlier; girls have to outperform their male counterparts to overcome being born as "weaker sex. A note of kudos for Indian girls – in spite of the lukewarm support from their so called "well-wishers", the "weaker sex" has excelled in every step of the societal ladder of 'excellence'; and number two – fighting the subtle derisions of being born as dark skinned. While dark skinned boys can hide behind the "dark and handsome" cliché, it's perhaps going to be another eternity before girls get such a break."

There was a total silence in the classroom. The students listened to him attentively.

Shrikant raised his hand again.

"Yes Shrikant," asked Prof. Srivastava, "Is there something you wish to add?"

"If it makes the *kaali* girls feel any better, I am regularly called names such as telephone, *habshi*, overcooked meat, *kajal*, carbon paper, and many others," added Shrikant.

The whole class laughed again. Prof. Srivastava joined the class and smiled with them.

"Would any girl like to comment?" asked Prof. Srivastava.

"Well, I've been called all those names too, plus some more such a *kaali ghata*, *kaali billi*. I guess I am just kind of used to it," said Sunita, "But, Professor -" she hesitated.

"Yes, go on," prodded Prof. Srivastava.

"What bothers me is that sometimes I feel that my parents are not very proud of me because of my dark skin. It seems as if they would be happier if I had lighter skin," continued Sunita.

"Well Sunita, I understand your predicament, but I don't think parents are any less proud of their children because of their darker skin. Parents have lived through color discrimination and they see it all around them. They are simply worried about what their children may experience because of what they recall from when they were younger. Sometime this concern about their children may unintentionally change parents' behavior towards their children," responded Prof. Srivastava.

Another lighter skin boy, DEV, 18, raised his hand.

"Yes Dev?"

"I don't have anything to add to color discrimination issue but I want to know why people color-discriminate?" asked Dev.

Prof. Srivastava pondered for a second and then responded.

"My answer in the context of Indian society is that 200 years of white British rule over Indians has eroded the self esteem of many of us and we have quietly accepted and perpetuated that white is superior, more intelligent, more beautiful than black. Also, if you recall the stories, we were told as children, often depicted evil, ugly, and unintelligent characters as being dark. Clearly we as a society have a long way to go to be completely color blind. But don't forget that we as a country are still going through adolescence having been independent for only 61 years. We are still learning and still trying to understand what it means to be not bossed around by white British. I believe education will help us reach there faster."

Prof. Srivastava checked his watch.

"We had an interesting discussion on this matter. We will continue with this topic on Monday," Prof. Srivastava continued, "Have a great weekend."

The class dispersed. Sunita was walking on the street behind a light skinned girl. There was a group of male students walking toward them. The light-skinned girl crossed the street in front of the boys and the group of males continued walking. A short distance behind the light skinned girl, Sunita crossed the street cutting in front of the males. One of the male students froze and held up his hands.

"Everebody freeze!" he yelled.

All the male students stopped in their tracks.

"Do you see that a *kaali billi* just crossed? It's a bad omen[2]," warned the male student making sure that Sunita heard him, "We need to have somebody else cross ahead of us. Otherwise it'll bring us bad luck."

Sunita scowled at the male students.

"Hey Suni, we're just teasing," said the male student laughingly.

"Very funny!" said Sunita angrily.

The male students all pointed to her and laughed making fun of Sunita's dark skin as Prof. Srivastava gazed on from his office window wondering if this problem would ever be solved.

---

2 It's considered a bad omen by some people in India if a black cat cuts in front of you.

CHAPTER III

Digital Artistry

Maya arrived home dripping with water. She opened the front door; put her umbrella and her shoes in a closet near the door. She called for Natasha while pacing toward her bathroom upstairs, "*Maa*, are you home?" Natasha called back from the kitchen.

"Yes. Let me change. I'll be right down there," responded Maya.

After changing, Maya walked into the kitchen where Natasha was preparing black tea. Maya inherited many beliefs during her upbringing on what causes skin color to become darker. One such belief was that drinking black tea or black coffee makes ones skin darker.

"Natasha, how many times I've asked you not to drink black tea? It's going to make your skin even darker. Whether you like it or not people care about it." Maya admonished her.

"The people who care don't matter, and the ones who matter don't care," responded Natasha, clearly irritated.

"Was it not Dr. Zeus who said something like it?" asked Maya.

"It was Dr. Seus, not Dr. Zeus," corrected Natasha.

Now, Natasha was by no means an ugly girl, infact most would consider her quite beautiful. At five feet seven inches tall and 120 pounds she would be considered an envy of most girls. There was only one problem that society saw in her: her skin color. Natasha had always wished for some form of relief from this burden, but after years of exposure and the realization that nothing could be done, Natasha had gotten used to her mother's constant chides on her dark skin color.

"I know you don't care but I do. Let me make some milk-coffee for you," said Maya as she dumped out Natasha's black tea into the sink and began to prepare some of her own.

"*Maa*, looking at the kind of things you buy into, nobody would believe that you're an educated bank executive," taunted Natasha.

"*Betey*, people have been following these traditions for ages. There has to be a reason for that," explained Maya, "Also, it's not going to hurt you if you listen to me."

"*Maa*, it is a bad thing to wish, but I wish you were colorblind," retorted Natasha.

Maya sideglanced at Natasha and smiled. "Ok, while you continue to wish that, please go and take a shower and put some makeup on yourself," said Maya, "I need you to look presentable so I can take some pictures of you."

"Why?" wondered Natasha, "Maa… NO. Are you going to send them to some prospective grooms?"

"Yes," replied Maya, "and there is nothing wrong with having your mother find you a husband. *Betey* you are 22 years old; if we don't marry you soon, it will difficult to find a good husband for you."

"*Maa*, my photographs have been rejected three times in last 6 months," Natasha reminded her mother, "How many times will you keep making me go through that?"

"Now Natasha, don't get disappointed. The only reason you are still alone is because of your skin color, and you have no control over that. You know, this is an unfortunate thing in our society that many people cannot still see beyond skin color," explained Maya while removing the milk coffee from the microwave.

Natasha could see the hypocracy in her mother's logic. She looked at her mother with amazement.

"*Maa*! I can't believe you're crictizing others for that when you wouldn't let me drink black tea for the same reason!" exclaimed Natasha.

Maya handed one cup of coffee to Natasha. "*Betey* calm down. I know what you are thinking," she said, "You are thinking that I discriminate based on skin shade, but I do not."

"Yes, you do *Maa*," retorted Natasha.

"No, I don't," Maya continued, "But I know that I live in a society that discriminates. What I am doing is to make sure people see beyond your skin color. Everything I do, I do because I want the best for you."

"Mother, do you remember what Gandhi said?" asked Natasha, annoyed at her mother's discriminatory nature.

Maya sideglanced at Natasha, "*Betey,* working full time and keeping tab on you, your father, and your long distance brother does not leave me any time to read about Gandhi?"

"Well *Maa*, what Gandhi said that 'you must be the change that you want to see in the world,' quoted Natasha, "and I completely agree."

"Sweetheart, I am not Gandhi," said Maya, "I am just trying to do what I think is best for my children. And mark my words - when you are in my situation, you will do the exact same."

"Never, not even in my wildest dreams," snapped Natasha as she shook her head disappointed that her mother thought so lowly of her.

"OK *Maa*. This discussion isn't going anywhere," said Natasha, "But you must agree that I'm a good daughter. None of my friends would ever let their parents do this to them."

Maya smiled and walked to her. She put her hand on her shoulders. "I know my darling. You are the best daughter any parent can ever wish for. And I wouldn't change you for the world," she said, "Now, like a good daughter, go and put on some makeup."

As Natasha huffed walking up the stairs, Maya heard the front door open.

"Hey guys, I'm home," called out Om.

Om hung his raincoat in the closet and walked straight into the kitchen.

"Go wash your hands; I'll make some coffee for you," Maya instructed Om.

"Oh yah, a cup of coffee would be great," said Om while walking away to wash his hands, "By the way, I talked to Mr. Mathur and told him that we would be emailing him Natasha's pictures today."

"Well…I thought about emailing her pictures but sometimes pictures on computer monitor may not look right," she replied.

Om stopped and turned toward her. "What do you mean?" he asked.

"If the computer monitor brightness is not set just right the pictures may look darker, and the Mathur's may not like that" she clarified.

"Oh, come on Maya, try not to be so judgemental," he bristled, obviously annoyed.

"Om, three boys have already said "no" to Natasha just based on her pictures. This time I want to do it right so she doesn't have to go through any more humiliation," she sputtered.

"Well whatever you do, please do it quick," said Om while washing his hands, "Mr. Mathur is expecting us to send him Natasha's pictures soon."

"Don't worry. I'll send her pictures today," she assured him.

Maya knew that Om was totally against offering any dowry to the boy's family in return for them to agree for the marriage, but she also knew the Mr. Mathur's son would be a great match for Natasha. She was willing to pay any price if it helped her daughter marry Mr. Mathur's son. She mustered courage to explore the dowry option with Om.

"Do you think we should somehow let Mr. Mathur know that we'll be open to giving dowry?" she probed him.

As soon as he heard the word "dowry" from her mouth, he felt as if his blood was boiling and instantly changed from a cheery professor to an angry father.

"Maaayaaa! I'll never buy off a man for my daughter," he screamed, "She'll never forgive me if I did that. Please!! Never suggest anything like that again. Natasha is good enough just the way she is, and I'll never even consider buying her a husband."

"OK, OK. Don't get angry," said Maya trying to calm him down, "But I don't want to miss a good match for her just because we did not want to pay."

"Maya, it is not that we don't want to pay. Don't you think it makes our daughter look cheap?" he continued, "It affects her self esteem. Natasha is such a talented and beautiful girl. If some boy can't see that then it is his loss"

He paused to take a breath. "And, as a matter of fact I don't want her to marry somebody who wants dowry," he continued, "Well anyway, this conversation stops right here. Please never again mention dowry."

"Ok, I won't talk about dowry again. Now calm down. I'll get you some coffee," she said.

There she sat, crying. Natasha had been in the bathroom for the last ten minutes and she had heard everything her mother had said. She liked to think that she was a strong and confident young lady, but when she heard her mother offer to buy her husband in belief that she could not get one on her own she just couldn't take it. Natasha slowly wiped the tears off her face and, with the strongest face she could muster, she descended down the stairs, ready for whatever was in store for her.

She proceeded toward her father who was still visibly agitated. She tried to change the subject. "*Pappa*, did you make an appointment with your doctor for your blood pressure check up," she asked.

Om looked at his daughter lovingly, able to see the faint signs of tears in her eyes. "Oh, it was a very busy day. I'll do it one of these days," he replied.

"That is it," declared Natasha, "I'm going to call the doctor tomorrow and set up an appointment for you."

"Don't worry, I'll call the doctor tomorrow," he reassured.

"Promise?" she asked.

He looked at her smilingly, "Yes, promise."

"And how is your presentation coming along?" he asked.

She took a deep breath. "I'm going to work on it tonight," she said.

Meanwhile, Maya put a tray with three glasses of milk coffee on the table, picked up her glass and headed upstairs to the computer room. Halfway up the stairs she looked at Natasha, "Natasha, will you please come upstairs. I need to take your pictures."

Natasha shook her head in frustration remembering the routine she went through several times before, and knowing that hoping for better eventual results would only lead to despair. Om lovingly patted his daughter on the shoulders encouraging her to put up with her mother for yet another time. Knowing there was nothing she could do, Natasha quietly followed her mother to Om and Maya's bedroom, knowing her mother would like to have a pre-photo make-up session to make sure Natasha looked as fair as possible.

As Natasha walked into the bedroom and saw her mother with the powder in her hand, she rolled her eyes, showing her irritation with her mother's obsession with skin color. But, she quietly agreed to let her mother work on her. They went to the adjacent bedroom where Maya did some facial touch up, and styled her hair.

"*Maa*, that is enough. I'm ready now," she protested, "You know it's not going to help. As soon as they find out about my skin color they will start getting cold feet."

"No my child, whoever you marry will be the luckiest man," Maya cajoled her.

Maya took out a bottle of a skin whitening cream to brush it on Natasha's face.

"*Maa*, I'm not going to put this junk on my face," she protested.

"You can wash it off after I take some pictures," suggested Maya.

"No *Maa*, it's not right," she asserted.

"Ok, Ok, don't put it on," Maya relented.

Maya had Natasha sit against a black backdrop in hopes that she would seem lighter, adjusted a couple of table lamps to brighten up Natasha's face and then took several shots of her.

"*Maa*, I've to prepare for my presentation. Can I leave now?" whined Natasha impatiently.

"I am almost done. Just hold on for a second," said Maya.

After Maya finished taking several more pictures, Natasha went to her room to work on her presentation.

Maya connected her camera to her laptop and transfered the pictures to her laptop. After the transfer, she looked at all the pictures one by one. She selected two pictures which appeared good and printed them. The printed pictures revealed Natasha's dark skin. She bolted her room door from inside while looking around to make sure that nobody was watching. She opened a photo-editing program and began to execute her plan of deception.

She digitally lightened up the skin. The screen showed Natasha's skin turning lighter. She printed the doctored pictures.

She looked at the printed pictures. She was still not satisfied with the lightness of the skin color. She returned to her computer and doctored the pictures some more hoping to make Natasha's skin look even lighter. Natasha now looked almost as if she was no longer Indian, but instead looked European. Satisfied with her now light-skinned daughter, Maya printed the photos, placed them in an envelope and took the envelope downstairs.

"Om, here are Natasha's pictures," said Maya, "Please mail them to Mr. Mathur tomorrow."

He took the envelope and placed it in his pocket without looking at the pictures inside.

"Thank you," he said, "Let me send Mr. Mathur an email."

"Ok," she said, "Meanwhile I'll get dinner ready."

He went to the computer room about to send the email. Several of Natasha's pictures were lying in the trash. He took the pictures out of the envelope and compared them with those that were in the trash. He immediately knew what Maya had done. He shook his head in bewilderment. He looked around to make sure that nobody was watching and then he removed the doctored picture from the envelope and replaced them with the pictures showing the true skin color of Natasha. He sealed the envelope and hid the light skinned doctored pictures in a closet.

"Everyone, come down. Dinner is ready," called Maya from downstairs.

"I'll be right there" both Om and Natasha answered in unison.

They walked down to the round dinner table. Maya had already arranged the food on the table. She was still in the kitchen making *rotis.* They sat across each other at the table.

"This looks like the same food we ate yesterday," commented Om.

"Yes, we need to finish the leftovers first," replied Maya from the kitchen.

"Maa, why don't you also join us?" asked Natasha.

"No, you guys go ahead. *Rotis* taste better when they are hot," replied Maya while bringing a batch of hot puffed rotis. She placed two rotis each on their plates.

"Don't forget to take salad. We need to finish it tonight," She instructed them while walking back to kitchen to make more *rotis*.

As instructed, they both served themselves salad – a mixture of cut cucumbers, onions, radishes, and carrots.

"Natasha *betey*, don't forget to email me your presentation slides tomorrow. I'll read it and give you my comments," Om reminded Natasha while munching on cucumbers.

"I'll try to finish it tonight," she replied.

"Can you pass the *baigan ka bharta* (mashed spiced roasted eggplant) please?" he asked Natasha.

She passed the bowl to him. He tasted it and liked the taste.

"The eggplant is really good," he said it loudly so Maya could hear it in the kitchen.

"Your daughter has made it," she told him proudly, "Whoever marries her will be the really lucky man."

Natasha smiled shyly. Om looked at Natasha affectionately.

"*Betey* Natasha, how am I going to live without you?" he asked, "I am going to let you leave this house only on one condition."

She looked at him curiously. "What is that?" she asked.

"I don't care how your *Maa* feels, but after you get married I'm going spend at least four months every year in your house," he announced.

"Only four months?" she joked.

"I love you my darling," he said with damp eyes.

She got up, walked around the table and hugged her father. Meanwhile, Maya brought another batch of fresh rotis.

"Where is my hug?" she asked.

Natasha smiled and walked up to her mother and hugged her.

They finished dinner and washed their hands. Natasha went back to the kitchen while Om went to the living room with a toothpick in his hand.

"Maa, you go and eat. I'll make fresh *rotis* for you," said Natasha.

"No, don't worry about it. I've already made enough for myself," replied Maya, "why don't you meanwhile put the dirty dishes in the sink.

After Maya finished her dinner, both Maya and Natasha walked into the living room where Om was strolling and still working with the toothpick.

He walked up the window to look outside. The sky had cleared. The rain had washed away the suspended smoke and dust particles that had filled the sky. He could see the moon and many bright stars.

"The rain has stopped. Who wants to come for a walk?" he asked.

"*Pappa*, I would love to come but I have to finish this presentation tonight," said Natasha.

Natasha turned to her mother. "*Maa*, you go with *Pappa*," she suggested.

"Ok, I'll go," said Maya.

"But, please don't forget to put the facial cream on before you go to sleep," reminded Maya.

Natasha again rolled her eyes in sarcasm.

"Yes *Maa*, I'll definitely not forget that. I mean, it'll help so much," she muttered.

They went out for a walk in a public park. The park was within a 5-minute walking distance from their house. It was a common place where people would come to get away from the hustle and bustle of crowded street traffic. Moreover, being surrounded by many trees, shrubs, and flowers beds, the park was perhaps the only place in their neighborhood where one could breathe air unadulterated with smoke and dust particles.

Om and Maya were still feeling quite emotional with the thought that Natasha was going to be gone soon and then there would be just two of them in the house without their children. They continued to walk on the narrow concrete walkway of the moonlit park.

"Vikram is already gone. I often get very scared thinking that soon somebody is going to steal Natasha from us," he said.

"I hope and pray that she finds a loving boy and family," he continued.

She nodded, "I hope so too. She is such a great kid."

"You know what scares me?" she continued.

"What?" he asked looking at her curiously.

"Sometimes I fear that she may not get what she deserves," she said.

"What do you mean?" he asked.

"It is her dark skin," she said.

She paused and then continued, "I feel guilty about it. And it is all because I made some mistakes."

Om knew where she was headed. "What mistakes?" he asked.

She took a deep breath.

"Remember 25 years ago when we were in Lucknow and I was pregnant with Vikram?" she recalled.

CHAPTER IV

Deep Roots

Maya was a 22-year old young woman when she was about one month pregnant with her first child. She rested on her bed reading a book on healthy pregnancy. She had started her work in a bank just a year ago which did not leave her much time to do much housework. She had hired a fulltime house maid to help her go through the pregnancy.

A lighter skinned house maid, Saraswati, 50, draped in an ordinary *sari* walked in with a cup of tea on a small tray.

"*Mem Sahib, Chaaye* (tea)," said the maid.

Maya looked up. "Saraswati, until I've had the baby please stop making tea for me. I am going to eat only yogurt and coconut," she instructed the maid, "And when you give me coconut, please make sure to scrape off the dark skin. I only want the white portion of the coconut."

The maid nodded in agreement. "*Mem Sahib*, this is the right thing you are doing," said the maid still holding the tray."

Maya put the book aside on a table next to her bed. "Why do you say that?" she asked curiously, though she was sure she already knew the answer.

Saraswati placed the tray on top of the dresser and took out two wrinkled pictures from under her blouse.

"See *Mem Sahib*, here are the pictures of my two daughters," said the maid while handing the pictures to Maya.

"You have beautiful children," said Maya with a smile.

The maid realized that Maya did not see the difference between her two daughters. "*Mem Sahib*, look at my daughters again," she clarified,

"The older one is completely dark-skinned but the younger one is not as dark."

Maya looked at the picture again. Sure enough, the difference in their skin color was remarkable. "Why is that?" she wondered.

"When I was pregnant with my first daughter, nobody told me about the proper techniques," explained Saraswati, "I drank tea everyday, and that too with buffalo milk, ate all dark colored food - and see what happened. Now my elder daughter's skin is very dark."

Maya was curious to know the whole story. "What about your second daughter?" she asked.

Saraswati continued, "After my first daughter was born, my friends told me to avoid dark colored food. Heeding their advice, I only drank cow's milk, and that too white cow's milk, ate a lot of coconut without its skin. And see, my second daughter is not dark." Maya nodded in approval, happy that she was not the only one who believed in this.

She continued, "*Mem sahib*, looking at the trouble I had to go through with my elder daughter's marriage, I know it does not matter much if you have a dark skinned boy, giving birth to a dark skinned girl leads to much hardship."

The maid took a deep breath. "The biggest problem was getting her married. No boy wanted to marry a dark-skinned girl. They all would want to marry my light-skinned, younger daughter," she said.

"What did you do then?" asked Maya.

Saraswati continued, "When a boy would come to see my elder daughter I would make sure that my younger daughter was not around. Still the only man who married her was darker than her and 20 years older than her too. Moreover, I had to give him all my savings in dowry. And even now, her in-laws always tease her about her dark skin."

"Do your daughters have any children?" asked Maya.

"Yes my elder daughter just had a girl," replied the maid, "God must be punishing us for some sins in our past life, because her daughter is even darker than she is."

"Didn't you tell her about the techniques you follow to produce a lighter skinned child?" Maya wondered.

Saraswati was a bit agitated, "*Arey Mem Sahib*, I told her everything, but every morning if she sees the face of her dark-skinned husband, how can she get a lighter skinned child. And everybody in her *sasuraal* (in-law's house) blames her for the dark skinned child. Her husband is also dark, but nobody blames him," she spoke with anger.

Maya tried to comfort her, "I pray to God to bring happiness to both your daughters. If there is anything I can do, please don't hesitate to ask."

"Thank you, *Mem Sahib*."

"Where does your elder daughter's husband work?" asked Maya.

"*Mem Sahib*, he pulls a rikshaw," Saraswati answered disappointedly.

Maya felt sorry for her and wanted to help her. "Do you want me to find him an employment in my bank?" she asked, "It'll probably pay more than what he makes now."

Maya could see Saraswati's face light up with the possibility of making a better life for her daughter. "*Mem Sahib,* that will be great! Perhaps, it'll make life a little better for my child," responded Saraswati ecstatically.

"Ok, send him to my office tomorrow," said Maya.

* * *

Nine months later Maya delivered a baby boy. As she looked at her child's glowing skin, Maya's heart jumped to a level of happiness she had never experienced before.

"See what a beautiful fair baby he is," she gloated at her son's skin color.

"Thank you God, you heard my prayers," she said while looking up toward heaven.

Om looked at his newborn son and smiled, "Thank you God for giving us a beautiful healthy child."

CHAPTER V

The Little Bowl

*** Three Years Later****

The moon was lighting up the night sky as Om and Maya's son, Vikram, sat on the bedroom floor playing with his toy truck.

Om was lying on his bed reading a book. Maya was at the dressing table putting some facial cream on her face while Vikram looked at her curiously.

"*Maa*, what are you putting on your face?" asked Vikram.

"*Beta*, this is a special facial cream," answered Maya with a smile while Om looked on.

Vikram asked again, "Why do you put it on your face?"

"It makes your skin color lighter," she answered.

"Why do you have to make your skin color lighter?" he persisted.

She was pleased with her son's curiosity but also a little frustrated with not being able to give him a convincing answer. "OK, Vickie you don't have to worry about it. You are the most beautiful *gora chitta* (white) boy. Give me a kiss and go to your room to sleep," she commanded, "And don't forget to brush your teeth before you go to sleep."

Vikram started to walk out of the room. Om was amused with his son's curiosity. He turned toward Maya. "Come on Maya, why don't you answer him?" he demanded, "Tell him why you have to lighten up your skin."

"Good night, Vickie," said Maya while ignoring Vikram.

"Good night *Maa*, Good Night *Pappa,*" said Vikram.

"Good Night," said Om.

The next day when Saraswati finished the house chores, she knocked at Maya's bedroom to talk to her.

"Come in," Maya answered.

She looked at her, "Yes Saraswati?"

"*Mem Sahib*, I've very good news," she said excitedly.

"I also have good news, but you tell me first," said Maya.

"*Mem Sahib*, my younger daughter is pregnant after a long time. She wants me to help her through this pregnancy so I'll have to be with her for about a year," Saraswati said.

Maya was also pregnant with her next child. As soon as she heard that she was concerned about not having Saraswati to help her during her own pregnancy. She knew that it would be difficult to find another maid as good as Saraswati.

Maya pleaded, "How will I manage without you?"

Saraswati showed her helplessness, "*Mem Sahib*, I'll have to go. It is a matter of just one year."

Maya pleaded again, "But I need you right now; I am again going to be a mother."

Saraswati was very happy to learn that Maya was pregnant again. "This is very good news," she said excitedly, "If you want I can talk to my elder daughter. She can work here."

Maya's anxiety decreased slightly. "Is she as good as you are?" she asked.

"She is very hard working. I've trained her well. You'll have no complaints," Saraswati said proudly.

"Ok, please do that, and take good care of your younger daughter," said Maya.

After Saraswati had left, Maya suddenly realized that the new maid was going to be dark skinned. She immediately shared her predicament with Om, "What do I do now Om?"

"What happened?" Om wondered.

Maya explained, "I don't understand Saraswati. She knows I am going to have another child. Why is she sending her daughter to work here?"

"What do you mean? She is just trying to help you," wondered Om.

Obviously, Om did not understand the consequences of having a black maid around. "Om, you don't understand. Her daughter is completely dark-skinned," she said irritatingly.

"So what?" snapped Om, "Her dark skin will not rub off our unborn child."

"I don't know how to explain it to you, but I don't want to take any chances," said Maya frustatingly.

Om tried to talk some sense into Maya, "Listen, it's very difficult to find a reliable maid these days. If you are concerned that, through some magical force, the dark color of her skin is going to rub off your unborn child, then I suggest that you don't come face-to-face with her until your delivery."

Maya was still very concerned but she did not see any way out of it. She reluctantly agreed to Saraswati's dark skinned daughter working in her house.

* * *

It was Kamla's first day of work at Srivastavas. As instructed by her mother, she prepared yogurt and coconut whites for Maya.

Meanwhile, Maya woke up, put on her gown and proceeded to the kitchen. As she entered the kitchen, she came face to face with Kamla. Maya hesitated with the sight of dark colored Kamla and immediately turned her face away and tried to walk out of the kitchen. When Maya was growing up, she was told by her mother that if you saw a dark skinned person first thing in the morning while you were pregnant, you tended to think about that person, and this in turn could trigger some reactions in your body which could cause you to give birth to a dark skinned child.

Kamla understood why Maya suddenely walked out of the kitchen.

"*Mem Sahib*, I did not know that you were coming here otherwise I would have covered my face," Kamla apologized.

Maya went back to her bedroom without responding to Kamla and woke up Om, "Om, can you please get me yogurt and coconut from the kitchen?"

"Why don't you ask Kamla?" wondered Om.

Maya was a little irritated for having to constantly defend her beliefs. "No, she is busy," she snapped, "Can you please go and get it?"

He reluctantly got up and went to the kitchen.

In the kitchen Kamla was standing there with her face covered in a long veil. Om sideglanced at Kamla surprisingly. He opened the fridge and took a yogurt bowl out.

She asked, "*Maalik*, do you want yogurt and coconut white for *Mem Sahib*?"

"Yes, but don't worry, I'll take it," he responded.

"No, *Maalik*, I've already made it for her. I know what she needs," she said.

Om put the yogurt bowl back into the refrigerator and instead took another bowl from Kamla. He then turned toward her. "Why are you covering your face?" he asked.

Kamla hesistated, "No reason *Maalik*."

Om shook his head in confusion. Then his eyes glanced over in the corner where a four year old dark skinned girl was sitting quietly.

"Kamla, is she your daughter?" he asked.

"Yes, *Maalik*," she replied.

He walked up to the girl and squatted in front her facing her. The little girl looked at him and smiled shyly.

"What is your name young lady?" he asked.

The little girl answered, "Radha"

"You know Radha, you are a very beautiful girl," said Om while gently poking her cheeks.

Radha looked at her mother and smiled shyly. Kamla smiled happily.

"So Ms. Radha, did you drink your milk this morning?" he asked.

Radha shook her head sideways in negative without saying anything.

Om then turned toward Kamla, "Kamla, give her also a glass of milk. And, not just today - everyday! The rule in this house is that you guys eat what we eat."

Kamla gestured her appreciation by smiling. "You are so kind and gracious," she said.

Om then leaned over Radha, "Drink a glass of milk and then go and wake up Vikram."

Om picked up the yogurt and coconut concoction for Maya and walked out of the kitchen looking at little girl smilingly.

Meanwhile, baby Vikram had just woken up and was already walking toward the kitchen while rubbing his eyes. Vikram entered the kitchen and looked at veiled Kamla. This was Kamla's first day of work and Vikram had never met her or her daughter before.

"Who are you?" asked Vikram.

"I am your new maid," replied Kamla.

He looked at her veil and wonderd, "Where is your face?"

Kamla unveiled herself and smiled, "Here it is, little master."

She bent down, put her hand on his shoulder. "I am going to take care of you, cook whatever you want, take you out for a walk, play with you, and tell you all kinds of stories," she told him smilingly.

He smiled and then looked to where Radha was sitting and writing something on a notebook.

"Who is that?" he asked.

"She is my daughter," answered Kamla.

He walked to the little girl and sat in front of her.

"What is your name?" he asked.

"Radha," answered Radha. "What is your name?" asked Radha.

"My name is Vikram," he answered, "My parents call me Vickki. You can also call me Vickki."

"My mom calls me *Gudiya* and my dad calls me Katori (an eating bowl)," Radha said shyly.

He was amused about the name Katori. He wondered why anybody would be named an 'eating bowl'.

"Why does your dad call you Katori?" he asked while giggling.

"When I was little I used to always walk with a little bowl in my hand always looking for something to eat, so my dad started calling me Katori," she explained.

"That's funny," he giggled again. Seeing him giggle, she also giggled.

Suddenly there was a concerned look at Vikram's face. "You have three names. I've only two. I'm losing," he said.

She giggled again.

He picked up a bowl from a shelf and gave it to her. He joked, "Katori, this is your *katori*."

Both of them giggled loudly. Kamla was amused seeing the two children having fun.

"I'll also call you Katori," he told her.

She gently touched his cheeks to feel them. "You are so white," she said admiringly.

Vikram remembered some of his mother's conversation with people about why he was so light skinned. He revealed the secret of his light skin, "You know, when I was in my mom's tummy, she drank a lot of milk and ate a lot of yogurt. That is why I'm white."

Nirmala looked at her mother and asked, "*Maa*, why didn't you drink a lot of milk and yogurt when I was in your tummy?"

Kamla's heart sank as she sensed the disappointment on her daughter's face about having dark skin. She tried to give it a positive spin, "*Betey*, I did not try that. But you know what? While you were in my tummy I prayed to God to give me a beautiful child, and God granted my wish."

Radha then turned to Vikram, "My dad says I'm the most beautiful girl. But I want to be white like you."

Even at his tender age of three years old, he could sense her new friend's sadness about her skin color.

"You don't worry; my mom has a cream. If you put that cream on your face you'll become white," he assured her.

"It doesn't work like that," she said.

"No, it does," he insisted, "My mom puts it on her face every day."

"Did your mom become white?" she asked.

"Not yet, but she'll become white one day," he answered.

Kamla interrupted their conversation, and brought a glass of milk to Vikram, "Here is your milk."

Without looking at the glass, he asked, "Did you put cocoa in it?

"Yes, I did put cocoa in it," answered Kamla.

He took the glass of milk and then turned toward Radha.

"Do you like milk?" he asked.

She quietly shook her head in affirmative.

"Then, why don't you also drink milk?" he asked again.

Kamla did not want to take advantage of Om's generosity. She understood the sensitivity of the situation. She was only a servant and Vikram was her employer's son, and thus her daughter was not entitled to everything that Vikram was.

She tried to intervene to handle the situation, "Little Master, you drink it; she'll drink it later."

He thumped his feet in protest, "No give it to her now. I want to race her to see who drinks it faster. I'll win, watch."

She realized that he was not going to take no for an answer. She relented, "Ok."

She took a much smaller glass and poured just a little milk in it and handed over to her daughter.

"You're cheating," he complained, "If you give her a small glass, she'll win. Give her the same size glass as mine."

Kamla smiled at his persistence. She gave another full glass of milk to Radha.

Vikram peeped into Radha's glass. Kamla had not put cocoa into Radha's glass. "You did not put cocoa into her milk," said Vikram while pointing to Radha's glass.

Before Kamla could answer Vikram, he gave Radha his own glass of cocoa milk and took Radha's glass and handed it over to Kamla.

"Put cocoa in this glass," he demanded.

Kamla was overcome with emotions to see this young boy's stubbornness for her daughter. She knew that her daughter rarely got to drink a full glass of milk, let alone the milk with cocoa. She took the glass and put cocoa in it. She gave the glass to him.

"Katori, you want to race?" he challenged her.

"OK," she accepted the challenge.

"When I say go, you start," he instructed.

He took a deep breath to get ready. Then he said "Ready, set, go."

He gulped it really fast. Radha, having never tasted cocoa milk before, hesitated a little in the beginning. But as soon as she began to drink, she started to savour the taste of cocoa milk. She forgot that she was in a race. Vikram won this race easily. He proudly showed off his empty glass to Radha while she was still enjoying her drink.

"I told you, nobody can beat me," he said triumphantly.

She was not sad about losing. She was enjoying the taste of her new drink.

Like a victorious matador, he proudly wiped his face with his shirt sleeves.

"Katori, how old are you?" asked Vikram.

"I'm four years old. How old are you?" she asked.

He raised three of his fingers, "I'm three years old."

"I'm one year older than you," she said.

"How do you know that?" he asked, dumbfounded at Katori's math skills.

She showed him by raising her four fingers, "See these four fingers? These are my four years."

He intently looked at her raised fingers.

She looked at him, "You're three years old, right?"

He nodded his head.

She continued, "Now you fold three of my fingers."

He folded three of her fingers one by one.

"Now how many fingers are left?" she asked smilingly.

"One," he said.

"See, it's simple. I'm one year older than you," she showed him.

"Wow. Do you know how to read?" he asked.

"Yes, I can read even the newspaper," she said proudly.

He could not believe it. "Really?" he asked, "Will you teach me how to read?"

"Yes," she said.

He did not want to wait. "Wait, let me bring my book," he said, "Then you can teach me."

He ran to his room to bring his book.

Meanwhile, Om was sitting on a desk grading students' papers. Maya was lying on her bed staring at the ceiling fighting an internal battle. She was fighting two conflicting struggles in her mind.

First, she suspected that her belief on how dark-skinned people could affect the skin color of her unborn child probably had no foundation.

Skin color is not like an infectious disease that will get transmitted to her unborn child. Her behavior toward her maid servant and her daughter must be debasing to them.

But on the other hand, the selfish mother within her who wanted nothing but the best for her unborn child wondered – what if the old beliefs and customs that she inherited from her mother were true. She remembered what her mother used to tell – "you need to eat right, be happy and think about good things while you are pregnant. Your thoughts control how your child will be." Then she reasoned – "If I am surrounded by dark-skinned people, they will be in my thoughts," she quickly saw the correlation between how the skin color of her unborn child may be affected by the skin color of people surrounding her during her pregnancy. "It's better to be safe than regret later, she reasoned in her mind, "She cannot take any chances. The stakes are too high. It may ruin her child's entire life. Besides, her maid servant understood the whole thing and supported her. She would not feel cast down. The maid servant's four-year old daughter may be too young to feel a sense of rejection. Besides, it would all be over in nine months."

In all her internal struggles, the selfish mother within her always found more reasons for her to perpetuate the beliefs that her mother had passed on to her.

Maya mustered enough courage to seek Om's help.

"Om, I know you will think I am crazy but until I deliver my child, please find some other maid," said Maya.

Om was peeved at Maya's beliefs. "Why, because she is dark skinned?" he retorted, "How can you believe in such stupid things?"

She was also not feeling too good about the whole situation. She was frustrtated that she could not make him understand what she was going through.

"Please don't argue with me, I don't want to take any chances," she pleaded again, "Just think about it. It's the future of our unborn child."

She continued, "I've chosen to go to work during off hours so I don't have to see any dark skinned person before my delivery. Every second I look at Kamla my baby's skin loses its fairness."

Om felt like pulling his hair out on this reasoning, but he knew this would aggravate the situation even more, and he should do everything to comfort her during her pregnancy in all possible ways.

He tried to keep calm. "Your reasoning does not make sense to me," he reasoned, "Besides, we cannot let her go. We have promised Kamla that we'll take care of her and her child's education. Not only that, Radha is a very smart and intelligent child. And using your reasoning, perhaps Radha's intelligence will rub off Vikram and do him some good."

She tried to settle down. "Om, I am really confused about this whole thing," she said, "Deep down in my heart I know that all this is just sheer nonsense. But due to my upbringing I keep hearing this voice that tells me not to take any chances. I don't know what to do. I need your help to get through this."

As Om tried to understand her mental struggle, Maya continued, "OK, let's do this. Until I deliver, you bring all my things from the kitchen. And tell Kamla to clean the house only when I am gone to work. I think she'll understand. I've already spoken with her."

He remained quiet.

She continued, "If Kamla was in my place, she would have done the same thing. I know all this does not make sense, but please let's not take any chances."

He reassured her, "Maya, it's bad for the baby when you are stressed. I'll do whatever you want, at least until your delivery"

"Thank you, Thank you, and Thank you. You are the greatest husband," she said.

He smiled, "I know that."

Meanwhile in the kitchen, Radha was teaching Vikram how to read when Om walked to the kitchen.

He greeted the children, "Good Morning Vickie. Hello again Radha."

Vikram was just too excited seeing that Radha could read.

Vikram ran to his father, "*Pappa*, Radha can even read the newspaper."

Om acted surprised, "Really, you aren't kidding?"

"No. Wait here, I'll show you," said Vikram excitedly.

Vikram quickly ran out to the living room and picked up a newspaper lying on the table and brought it. He gave the newspaper to Radha.

"Katori, show him that you can read newspaper," he said.

Radha looked at the newspaper and then looked at Vikram, "Which part do you want me to read?"

He randomly pointed at a news article, "Read this one."

Om was getting amused. Kamla stood at another end of the kitchen looking at them curiously.

Radha read the news article in broken English. While Radha read the newspaper, Vikram proudly looked at Om trying to show off Radha's brilliance. Om acted totally impressed at Radha's feat.

"I don't believe this. This is just amazing," said Om showing his amazement.

Vikram proudly smiled as if it was his own achievement.

"Can she teach you how to read?" Om asked.

"She is already teaching me," said Vikram.

"That is great!" said Om, "Ok you guys continue working on your reading skills. I'll get some apples for your mother."

"Kamla, can you please cut some apples for Maya?" asked Om.

"I'll do it right now," replied Kamla.

"Kamla, I want to apologize on behalf of Maya," said Om.

"Apologize for what?" she inquired.

"You know her belief about seeing the dark skinned people."

Kamla interrupted him, "Don't worry about it. In fact if I were in her situation, I would have done the same thing."

"You know all these things are totally baseless," said Om.

"May be *Maalik*, but why take any chances," Kamla countered with the same argument that he heard before.

Om shook his head. "You sound so much like Maya," he said.

Kamla smiled as she watched Om leave.

Radha was still helping Vikram learn how to read.

"Katori, do you watch TV?" asked Vikram.

"We don't have TV in our house," answered Radha, "Sometimes I watch at my neighbor's house."

He was surprised to learn that she did not have a TV. "You don't have a TV in your house?" he asked with his eyes wide open.

"No," answered Radha.

He got up and held her hand, "Do you want to watch TV in my room?"

She looked at her mother. "Mamma, can I go to his room?" she asked.

"Ok, but promise me that you'll not go to *Mem Sahib's* bedroom," instructed Kamla.

"I promise," she assured.

"Why can't she come into *Maa's* room?" asked Vikram, "Don't worry, she'll not break anything. My Mom is very nice, she'll not be angry."

Kamla secretly signaled Radha and with her pointer finger reminding her to not go to Maya's room. Radha got her mother's signal and nodded her head.

Vikram took her to his room. She stood near the door and gaped at his room in amazement. There were so many things there - a beautiful bed, a desk, a micky mouse table lamp, a bookshelf packed with colorful books, a closet packed with clothes, many toys scattered around the room, and much more... She could not help but to think what she had in comparison - She didn't have any of these things; she didn't even have her own room;

she slept with her parents on a small squeaky wooden cot; she did all her school work on floor.

"This whole room is yours?" she asked in amazement.

"Yes, this whole room is mine," he said proudly.

"Where is your TV?" she asked.

He led her to his desk, "Here it is."

She looked at his TV and his room admiringly.

"Do you want to watch it?" he asked.

She wanted to say yes, but she suddenly remembered something. "No, not now," she said, "I've not finished my homework yet."

Noticing that she was impressed with the size of his room, he wanted to impress her even more by showing off his parents' room, "OK, come on I'll show you my Mom and Dad's room. Their room is even bigger than mine."

He ran upstairs to his parent's room. She followed him hesitatingly. As soon as she reached the bedroom door, she remembered that her mother had told her not to go to Maya's bedroom.

He opened the bedroom door and walked inside but she stayed outside.

"Katori, come inside," he said.

"No, my mother told me that I'm not allowed to come in front of *Mem Sahib*," she said.

He did not understand why she was not allowed.

Meanwhile Maya noticed Vikram at the door. "*Betey* Vicky, what are you doing? Come to me," she said.

"*Maa*, Katori is not coming in," said Vikram, "She says she is not allowed to come in front of you. Please call her in."

Maya was deeply agonized by this. "Oh God, I don't want to poison this little girl's tender mind," she muttered to herself, "Please help me God."

Om's concentration was broken by this. He could not continue grading the papers while all this was going on. He turned around in his revolving chair and stared at Maya. He was visibly enraged.

At the same time, from downstairs, seeing Radha standing in front of Maya's bedroom, Kamla panicked. She tried to take control of the situation and immediately called out for Radha, "*Gudiya*, I'm leaving. It's time for your school. Come down quick otherwise you'll be late."

Radha remembered again that she had yet to finish her homework. She panicked, "Oh my God, I've not finished my homework yet." She ran downstairs to the kitchen.

Om watched all this in frustration. He could not take this anymore. He bolted from his chair and strode downstairs to the kitchen.

"Kamla, you go home. I'll drop Radha to her school. And I'll do this every day," declared Om, visibly upset.

"No *Maalik*, I can take her," she said politely, "There is plenty of time."

"I know that. But she has not done her homework. I'll drive her to school so she can do her homework in the car," he insisted.

"Come on young lady, I'll take you to school," he said while extending his hand to her, "And I'll take you to school everyday."

Radha looked at her mother asking for her permission to go with Om. Kamla smiled and nodded slightly.

Vikram also ran down to the kitchen behind his father. "*Pappa*, can I also come with you?" he asked.

"Yes, come on, let's go," replied Om.

Om turned toward Radha. "Radha, pick up your school bag, let's go," said Om.

Radha and Vikram left with Om.

Unaware with the commotion downstairs, Maya sat in her room very frustrated about the situation. She was again torn between the two mindsets. She knew that she could make Kamla understand her situation, but could this little girl Radha understand this? She struggled with these thoughts for a few seconds and then suddenly she could not take it anymore. She sprang up from her bed and rushed out of the room and started calling for Kamla from upstairs balcony.

"Kamla, where are you?" yelled Maya.

As Kamla saw Maya coming out of her bedroom, she immediately covered her face so Maya did not have to see her dark face.

Maya came downstairs to kitchen where Kamla was standing with her face covered.

"Kamla, I can't let your little girl go through this. She should not grow up believing in this nonsense. Where is she? I'll take her to her school," exclaimed Maya.

Kamla knew that Maya was overcome by emotions. She tried to calm her down, "*Mem Sahib*, what are you doing? Your little rash behavior will make you regret it for the rest of your life. Please don't worry about anything, we don't feel bad about you not seeing our dark faces."

Kamla continued to put Maya at ease, "If I had taken precautions when I was pregnant with Radha, she would have been a *gori* girl. Please don't make the mistakes I made. If it's causing so much of a problem, and if you trust us, you can give us the house key. Then I can do all the housework when you are not here, and leave before you return."

"Kamla, these are useless beliefs," countered Maya agitatedly, "I cannot let these children grow up with this crazy idea. I cannot do this. I cannot do this."

Kamla continued to calm Maya, "*Mem Sahib*, don't worry about it. My daughter is very understanding. I've told her everything and she does not feel bad about it."

"You go to your room, please, *Mem Sahib*," pleaded Kamla.

Maya was still flustered, but a little less agitated. Whatever Kamla said was making sense to her. "Kamla, I don't know what to do," she moaned.

"*Mem Sahib*, just do what I am telling you," suggested Kamla, "From tomorrow onwards I'll come after 10 O'Clock and finish all the house work. You just leave everything to me until your pregnancy. You just watch, your child will be as white as an *Angrezi babu* (a white boy) or *Angrezi Mem Sahib* (a white girl)."

The thought of having a white child put Maya in a sweet fantasy and she immediately forgot about the mental torment she was going through just a few moments ago. The anticipation of having another fair child put a smile on her face. She was suddenly very calm.

"OK, let's do this. I'll change my office hours and I'll go at 7:30 am. So you can come at 8:00, provide food to Om, take care of the housework," suggested Maya.

Kamla reassured her, "Everything will be OK, *Mem Sahib*. It's just a matter of nine months. We will manage that."

Maya was very appreciative of Kamla's understanding of her situation, "Kamla, God bless you. God has sent you especially for me. I am so thankful to you,"

Kamla responded humbly, "*Mem Sahib*. I am not doing anything for you. It is you who has done so much for me and my family. You provided employment to my husband and now you have given me and my daughter your support. I'll always be grateful to you."

Maya smiled and went back to her bedroom.

CHAPTER VI.

Congratulations?

*** Nine Months Later ***

"Go and call the doctor, I think she is ready to deliver," told the head nurse to her assistant.

The assistant nurse ran out and returned with a doctor. To Maya's delight, the doctor was also a light skinned 35 year old woman.

Suddenly, panic set in; the medical instrumentation started to beep. Then, one of the nurses monitoring baby's heart beat monitor screamed.

"Doctor, something isn't right with the baby's heartbeat."

The doctor panicked. She tried to do something under the covers but panic still persisted. The heart monitoring instrument started to beep louder.

"Run and and call Dr. Vyas quick," shouted the doctor.

The nurse ran outside and returned with a very dark skinned middle aged lady doctor.

Maya got a glimpse of her and quickly turned her head away and closed her eyes.

Dr. Vyas looked at the readings and then examined Maya under the cover. Everybody looked on anxiously and nervously. Dr. Vyas did a few things under the cover. The beeping stopped slowly. The baby's heart beat came back to normal.

"Let's continue to monitor her for about 10 minutes and then we will deliver the baby," instructed Dr. Vyas.

Dr. Vyas washed and wiped her hand and approached Maya. As soon as Maya saw her she moved her head away from the doctor and closed her eyes pretending to be in terrible pain. Dr, Vyas put her hand on Maya's head to comfort her.

"Hi, I am Dr. Meghna Vyas. Don't worry, everything is OK. It was just the entangled umbilical cord. Your child is completely healthy," said Dr. Vyas, "I want you to relax for a few minutes and then we will deliver the child."

Maya did not respond to her. She continued to keep her eyes closed.

Dr. Vyas thought that she was in terrible pain that was why she did not pay attention to her.

Dr. Vyas turned toward the head nurse. "I'll be in the next room. Please monitor her blood pressure, child's heart rate and if there is anything unusual call me immediately," instructed Dr. Vyas.

Outside of the delivery room, Om was pacing the hallway wondering what was happening with Maya.

Dr. Vyas approached Om, "Are you Maya's husband?"

"Yes, Doctor," he answered nervously.

"Mr. Srivastava, I am Dr. Vyas and I am looking after your wife. There was a little panic situation. The umbilical cord got tangled up a little," she informed him.

"Are Maya and the child ok?" he asked nervously.

"Yes, yes, everything is under control. Both the mother and child are perfectly fine," Dr. Vyas reassured him, "But if there was a little delay, the lack of oxygen to child's brain could have been fatal for both mother and child."

"Are you sure, both of them are ok?" he asked again.

"Yes, Yes, I assure you that your wife is ok and you are going to have a perfectly healthy child," replied Dr. Vyas.

Inside the delivery room, Maya was still in pain. She continued to close her eyes not knowing where Dr. Vyas was. After a few seconds, once she realized that the doctor had left the room, she squint opened her eyes to make sure that the doctor was not there.

Maya signaled one of the nurses to come to her. The nurse approached her.

"Excuse me, can you please call my husband," she requested, "He is outside in the waiting area."

A few seconds later, the nurse returned with Om.

He approached Maya. She gestured him to come close to her face. He bent down to bring his ear near her.

"Om, did you the see doctor?" she whispered into his ears.

"Yes I talked to her. Why?" he wondered.

Inspite of being in extreme pain, she was still concerned about her child's skin color.

"Did you see how black she is? Please find me another doctor otherwise all precautions that I took for the past nine months will go waste," she pleaded.

He bristled at her suggestion, "Are you out of your mind! This is an emergency situation. If she was not here you and your child's life could have been in danger."

She pleaded again, "I beg you, please do something."

He tried to calm her down, "You are about to deliver and you want me to find another doctor? Just try to relax for yourself and your soon to be born child. Everything will be fine."

She feared the worst. He pulld a chair and sat near her and started rubbing her head.

Meanwhile Dr. Vyas walked in.

"How are we doing?" Dr. Vyas asked the nurses.

"Doctor, I think she is ready," replied the head nurse.

After a few moments, cries of a new born child were heard. The doctor picked up the baby girl and handed her over to one of the nurses to clean her. Maya could not yet see the girl because the bedsheet covering her blocked her view. Maya tried unsussessfully to get the glimpse. Om could see the child. The girl was dark-skinned.

"Congratulation Mom and Dad! It's very beautiful and healthy girl," announced the doctor.

Maya was still in pain, but she managed to signal Om to come closer to her.

"What is her skin color?" she whispered to him.

He patted her head. "She is very beautiful," he told her, knowing how distressed she would be if she knew the child was dark-skinned.

Meanwhile the nurses cleaned up the baby. A nurse wrapped the baby in a blanket and went to the corner of the room to weigh her. Maya unsuccessfully tried to get the glimpse of her skin color. Through the space between nurses Maya tried to see her daughter's skin color. She mistakenly thought that the nurse's white arm was baby's leg. Maya's face immediately started to glow with happiness. She looked up in the sky, and thanked God.

"The weight of the child is seven pounds. She is 18 inches tall," announced the nurse.

The nurse handed the baby over to Dr. Vyas. The doctor walked to Maya with the wrapped baby girl.

"Mom, are you ready to see your beautiful daughter?" asked Dr. Vyas smilingly.

She put the child in Maya's lap. Only a small portion of child's face, her nose and mouth were visible. Maya could not hide her joy in anticipation of seeing a lighter skinned child.

Dr. Vyas smilingly handed over the child wrapped in a towel.

Maya first looked at the exposed dark nose of the child. The expressions on her face slowly began to change from happy to panic. Using her fingers she quickly exposed a little more of her child's face. Om understood the delicacy of the situation. Dr. Vyas looked on smilingly at Maya's face. Not believing the child's skin is dark-colored, Maya quickly uncovered child's entire face. Maya's face quickly changed from panic to blank. She looked at the doctor.

"Doctor, her skin…," stuttered Maya.

Dr. Vyas interrupted Maya thinking that Maya was concerned that the girl was not cleaned well.

"Don't worry about it now, once the nurse gives her a good bath she'll look much cleaner."

Maya looked at Om helplessly and expected Om to do something. He understood what she was thinking and tried to take control of the situation.

"She is so beautiful," he said while touching the baby's cheeks lovingly.

"OK…," the doctor spoke with a confused tone not being able to understand Maya's reaction to the baby, "Congratulations to both of you and enjoy your beautiful daughter," said Dr. Vyas while leaving the room, "I will be in my office. Please let me know if you need anything."

The nurses left the room leaving Om, Maya and their newborn daughter in the room.

Meanwhile at Om's house, Vikram, Kamla and Radha were at home anxiously waiting near the phone for the good news.

"*Chotte Sarkar* (little master), why don't you call hospital to see if everything is OK?" asked Kamla.

Vikram dialed the number for the hospital

Om picked up the phone.

"*Pappa*, did the baby come out from *Maa*'s tummy?" asked Vikram.

"Yes, a very beautiful baby came out of *Maa*'s tummy," said Om laughingly, "Now you are big brother of a beautiful sister."

Vikram looked at Radha. "Katori, I'm a big brother. I've a little sister," he announced excitedly.

Kamla was very anxious and restless. She wanted to know more details about the baby, especially her skin color. "*Chotey Sarkar*, let me talk to your *Pappa*?" she asked.

He handed over the phone to Kamla.

"*Maalik*, is everything ok?" she asked.

"Yes, everything is just fine," answered Om, "Maya just delivered a beautiful baby girl."

Kamla was keen to know about baby's skin color but she hesitated to ask Om.

"Can I talk to *Mem Sahib*?" she asked.

Om handed over the phone to Maya and gently took the baby from her.

He sat on the rocking chair next to Maya's bed and started doing the baby talk with the little girl.

Maya's face was a still blank with mixed emotions. She took the phone and tried to control her emotions.

"Kamla, something went wrong somewhere," Maya sobbed.

"*Mem Sahib*, what happened?" she asked dreadfully.

"Something went wrong somewhere," Maya repeated.

Kamla could not control her anxiety, "*Mem Sahib*, please tell me what happened. Is everything Ok?"

"My daughter is not *gori* (white)," revealed Maya.

Kamla clinched her eyes. There was a silence at both ends of the telephone. After a few moments she collected herself. "*Mem Sahib*, you don't worry," she consoled her, "Whatever God does, there is always a reason for that."

"*Mem Sahib*, now you come back home quickly," she continued, "I'll use whitening cream on her everyday and you just watch, her skin will be glowing in no time,".

Om tried to make Maya feel relaxed by gently squeezing her hand. "Thank you for giving us a beautiful daughter," he said, "You did very well. You are a very brave woman."

CHAPTER VII

Illogical Logic

Om and Maya were sitting on a bench in the park. She just finished reliving the period when her daughter was born.

"Yes, I am a brave woman. See the result of my bravery?" she derided herself.

"What result?" asked Om.

After a deep breath, she explained, "Natasha's skin color; It has been 20 years, and I've never forgiven myself for my actions. If I had followed the customs and beliefs that our ancestors have been following, my daughter would have been lighter skinned too."

Om tried again to challenge her, "Maya, this is all nonsense. How can you believe in things like these?"

"Then, how do you explain that Vikram is so light-skinned and Natasha is so dark?" she asked.

Om did not see much logic in her reasoning. He tried another spin, "Maya, the biology of pregnancy works in a complex manner and I don't think I am qualified to give you a convincing answer, but I can guarantee that the child's skin color is NOT determined by whom you see during your pregnancy." He continued after a pause, "And even if it does affect, then what is wrong with having a dark skin color. Our daughter is beautiful; she is smart, intelligent, and caring. Is that not a reason to celebrate and feel lucky? Your unfounded guilt must make Natasha feel a lesser human being. I am sure she can see that guilt in your eyes."

"Inspite of her dark skin, I've never loved her any less than Vikram," she continued to defend her belief.

Om suddenly got upset and his voice became a little louder, "Maya, please don't say 'in spite of her dark skin'. It sounds like that she does not deserve your love and you are doing a big favor to her."

"I am sorry. I did not mean that," she apologized realizing how her statement would be interpreted.

"Also Maya, love is not like a light switch that you turn on and off at will," he asked, "If you are constantly being eaten up by this stupid guilt, how can it not show in your behavior towards Natasha?"

She was speechless and looked up blankly.

"I hope and pray that she does not have to go through the same discrimination as I did," she sobbed.

Om continued with his barbs, "You expect others to not discriminate against your daughter when you yourself are discriminatory?"

Maya sat quietly without making eye contact with Om. She did not want to let go of her beliefs, but at the same time she was unable to repond to Om's reasoning effectively. Her eyes were a little damp.

Noticing her damp eyes, he calmed down and tried to act like a teacher explaining a tough problem to a student. "If there is color discrimination in USA, I can understand it because whites and blacks are from different races, they have different histories, and they have different appearances," explained Om, "But look at us Indians, we look similar, have similar backgrounds, and are the same race. What reasons do we have to discriminate among our children?"

"I love both of my children equally," she said while defending her love for her children.

"Perhaps you do, but your constant guilt about being responsible for her darker skin may have a risk of blurring your love for Natasha," Om retorted.

"Natasha is smart and mature enough to be not affected by this," countered Maya.

"OK, so we have established one thing that you are not as smart and mature as your daughter," he said while smiling.

Om's remark brought a slight smile on her face. She quipped back, "Perhaps I am not, but I would like to take credit for giving my daughter a good training."

Meanwhile, Om's cellphone rang.

"Yes Natasha. What is it?"

"*Pappa*, where are you guys?" asked Natasha.

"Betey, we are coming in few minutes. Your *Maa* and I were involved in deep intellectual conversation," explained Om.

"You can continue the conversation at home. Please come soon, it's almost 10 O'Clock," Natasha pleaded.

"We'll be there in a few minutes," he answered as they began the trek back home.

CHAPTER VIII

Color Blind Love

Vikram lived in the United States working as a software project manager. As he finished his work, he decided to make a call to his girlfriend Megan, another computer executive living in the United States.

"Hi Vikram, are you done for the day?" answered Megan.

"Yes I'm, how about you?"

"I can be done if you have some tempting alternative," teased Megan.

"How about you join me for some spicy Indian dinner tonight at Bombay Palace?" proposed Vikram.

"That sounds tempting," said Megan.

"Ok, I'll go home, call my parents, take a shower and then pick you up at 6:30," he told her.

"That sounds great," said Megan, "I'll see you soon."

Vikram collected his briefcase. Another of his colleague and a friend of his, Mohan, walked into his office.

"Hi Vikram"

"Hi, Mohan"

"Do you want to go for a beer tonight?" asked Mohan.

"I'd love to, but I'm meeting Megan for dinner at Bombay Palace," said Vikram, "But you're welcome to join us."

"Oh, really?" taunted Mohan.

"Why not," said Vikram, "I'll try to get not too romantic with Megan."

"If you say so," mocked Mohan.

Mohan did not want to be a spoiler in Vikram's romantic evening with Megan, "No, I'll let you two love birds have quality time with each other. I'll catch you some other day. By the way, how is the family in India?"

"They are great. I'll be calling them when I get home," said Vikram.

"Say hi to them from my side," said Mohan.

"I sure will," replied Vikram.

Vikram put his laptop in the bag and walked out of his office. "Hey," said Vikram to Mike, another colleague of his, "How did the meeting with Microsoft go?"

"I think it went very well. Let's keep our fingers crossed," said Mike, "Thanks for the slides that you provided. In fact they were more interested in the material you provided. It's possible that you may get a call from them."

"Great. Let's hope we get the contract," said Vikram,"We'll talk about it some more tomorrow."

Vikram drove home and entered his apartment. He put down his laptop and called home."

Maya was always excited hearing from Vikram - "Oh, *beta* Vickie. How are you?"

"I'm good. I hope I did not wake you up?" said Vikram.

"No, you know that I wake up early. What time is it there?" she asked.

"It's about 5:30 pm," answered Vikram.

"Did you eat your dinner?" she asked.

"No, I'm going to eat at an Indian restaurant with a friend."

"Who, Mohan?" she wondered.

Vikram had never told his mother about his relationship with Megan. He was not sure if she would approve. He paused for a second and said hesitatingly, "Yes, Mohan."

Maya knew Mohan's parents who lived near her house in India. She was pleased about Vikram's friendship with Mohan. "We ran into his parents at the bus stop yesterday," she said, "They are nice people. They have invited us for dinner on next Saturday."

Vikram felt uneasy about lying to his mother. He tried to change the subject, "That is great. How is your cold *Maa*?"

"Oh it was not a cold; there was something that I ate which made my throat itch," Maya clarified.

"Are *Pappa* and Natasha sleeping?" asked Vikram.

"Yes, they are still sleeping. Shall I wake them up?"

"No, don't wake them up. I'll call later," he said.

One of Maya's main dreams was – to marry her son to a girl of her choice. Knowing that he was preparing to leave, she quickly came to the point, "*Beta*, I am getting a lot of marriage proposals for you. Some of these girls are really nice."

Vikram joked and again tried to change the subject, "*Maa*, can I marry all of them?"

Maya laughed, "No *beta*, marriage is a very sacred union between one man and one woman. Stop kidding and tell me when you're coming back here?"

"*Maa*, I don't know yet. I'm busy right now," he said feeling uneasy with the conversation on this subject.

"*Beta*, try to find some time. I want to see you," she pleaded, "It has been almost two years since I saw you."

Vikram knew that his mother was missing him. He tried to comfort her – "You see me on video chat."

"I know that but it's not the same," she said.

He looked at his watch. He was supposed to be picking up Megan in a few minutes. He always bragged to Megan about his time punctuality habit and how he hated those who are not on time. He must wrap up this conversation with his mother - "I'll try my best to get some time off," he said hurriedly, "OK *Maa*, I've to go and pick up Megan."

"Pick up who?" wondered Maya.

Vikram realized the slip, "Úmm… pick up Mohan"

"It sounded like you said Megan," she said.

"No, *Maa* I said Mohan," said Vikram trying to undo the damage.

"Perhaps the old age is affecting my hearing," she responded.

"You're not that old and you're not losing your hearing," he said, "OK *Maa*, I'll call you later. Bye."

"Bye *beta*."

Vikram took a deep breath, hung up the phone, and wonderd what would have happened if his mother had found out about his relationship with Megan.

CHAPTER IX

The Tipping Point

It was morning time. Maya was already up and she was doing her morning *pooja*. Om and Natasha had just woken up. Suddenly there was a power outage in the house. The lights went off. Natasha was brushing her teeth in her bathroom when it suddenly turned dark. She immediately paused brushing and tried to remember if she had saved her presentation before she went to bed. With her toothbrush in her mouth, she sprinted to the computer room. The computer room was also dark. She looked at her the computer and murmured to herself, "I hope I saved my presentation slides last night."

She continued to pace back and forth near the computer fearing the worst and hoping for the best. After a few minutes the power came back on. She quickly turned the computer on and tried to find the file she was working on.

"NO!" she screamed.

Om heard her scream and came running to the computer room.

"What happened?" he asked.

Natasha was sitting in front of the computer holding her head down with the toothbrush sticking out from the side of her mouth.

"You'll not believe *Pappa*, how stupid I'm," she said frustatingly.

"What happened?" he asked.

She put her hands on her head in fruatration, "I did not save my work on the computer last night, and this power failure killed all what I did. What a moron I am. I worked on it for at least two hours," she revealed.

"When is the presentation due?" asked Om.

"Day after tomorrow," she responded nervously.

Om put his hand on her shoulders and tried to encourage her – "Don't worry, we'll work together on it tonight and finish it," he continued, "By the way, on the same note, I kind of agree with you when you said you are such a moron, especially considering that power outage is a common occurrence in this town."

Natasha, still frustrated, murmured, "You're right, I'm such an idiot!"

Natasha was quite irritated at herself. Om went back to his bathroom. Maya was still busy doing *pooja,* oblivious of the disaster the power outage had caused on Natasha.

Om was almost ready to go to work, while Natasha was quietly sitting at the breakfast table, still irritated.

"Cheer up, girl! We'll fix your presentation tonight," said Om while walking out the door, "I'll see you in the evening."

As Om left to go to work, Natasha sat alone on the breakfast table. To lessen her anxiety, she made herself some black tea. As she took the first sip, Maya walked in after finishing her *pooja*. She could not stand the sight of Natasha drinking black tea. "In spite of her reminding Natasha about the perils of black tea, she continued to drink it," wondered Maya. She could not control herself and lost her temper. "N-a-t-a-a-sh-a-a-a-a! How many times I've told you not to drink black tea until you get married," she screamed, "Can you just follow one thing that I tell you? I am afraid that you have been drinking black tea when I am not around, that is why there is not any change in your skin color!"

Natasha was already in a bad mood. She snapped back angrily with her voice raised, "*Maaaaa*...., please stop being ashamed of me! It's not like if I drink water my skin will become see-through, or if I drink orange juice my skin will become orange! I know that three boys have already rejected me but I don't care. I'm happy the way I look. If nobody marries me, that is fine too. I can take care of myself. Now please leave me alone!"

Maya was stunned. She had never seen Natasha snap like this before.

"What did you say? What did you say? I am ashamed of you?" she demanded an explaination for that statement.

Natasha's voice was still raised, "Yes *Maa*, you're ashamed of me. Don't try to deny it!"

Maya's anger suddenly changed into sadness. Her eyes got a little damp at Natasha's outburst, and in particular, her accusation.

"Oh my child how can you say that?" sobbed Maya, "The only reason I am doing this so you don't have to go through what I went through."

Natasha was carrying many years of grudge against her mother's obsession with skin color. Combined with her irritated state of mind, the grudge reached the tipping point today. She continued with her barrage, "What are you talking about, *Maa*? You had a wonderful life with *Pappa*. But for some reason, you believe deep down in your heart that dark skin is something to be ashamed of. I'm not ashamed of my skin color. I'm a confident and successful girl. It's you who continue to remind me that I'm a lesser human being. I'm perfectly happy with myself"

Maya was quietly sobbing at Natasha's outburst. There was a pause and then Maya spoke, "*Betey* when I was 17 years old you could not imagine what I had to go through..."

CHAPTER X

Deep Scars

"The suffering I went through started 33 years ago"

I had just turned 17, and my mother was dressing me up for a visit with a prospective groom. My younger sister, Sapna, was helping my mom with the decorations. Sapna looked almost my twin, except that at 5 feet 4 inches she was about one inch shorter than me; but she had what counted the most - she had much lighter skin. Mom was dressing me up so that the least amount of my skin was visible. She put a lot of make up on my face to hide my dark skin.

I would argue with her – '*Maa*, the times have changed. People are not as conservative as they were in your time.'

She would cut me off by saying, 'This is what I used to tell my mother. I knew it then and I know it now, people have not changed, nor will they ever change.'

Perhaps the worst part of my mother's obsession with marriage was its effect on my schooling. The prospective groom's family would always want to meet during the day, and since that conflicted with school, my mother would always make me miss school to meet them.

Every time I would plead, '*Maa*, don't make me miss school again.'

But she would ignore me and respond by saying, 'Don't worry about school. If you get a good husband you'll never have to work.' And no matter what I did there was no way to make her change her mind even though Sapna and I both loved school and were actually top students.

Anyway, while I was sitting getting ready, the doorbell rang. Mom got very excited, and called for my father, 'Listen, this must be the boy's family,' my mom said as I sat there like a doll, 'Can you please get the door? I'll bring Maya in a minute.'

Just as my mom had suspected the groom's parents and the prospective groom had arrived and I was ready to be put on display. Once the groom and his family were seated my mom called for Sapna to enter, and after a few minutes I was slowly paraded into the living room.

I sat next to the boy's mother, but I could clearly see that the boy's mother was surprised because she was expecting Sapna to be the one they were seeing. Also it seemed as if she was a little suspicious of me because I was all covered up. She gave me a quick look then realized that my fingers were exposed, and by asking me to pass the coffee she realized my fingers, and therefore my skin was dark. And thus my turn was over.

Instead of focusing on me, the groom's mother seemed like she was more interested in Sapna. She turned toward Sapna and politely asked her, 'What is your name betey?'

'Sapna.'

The boy's mother smiled to show her liking for Sapna, 'It's a very sweet name.'

Sapna just smiled. My parents felt a little awkward by the groom's mom's lack of interest in me and interest in Sapna. Suddenly my mother intervened, 'My daughter Maya is very proficient in household work and very good in studies. She has won many awards for being a top student. Betey Sapna, why don't you go and get her trophies.'

Sapna went inside to get some of my trophies and certificates.

But, the groom's family was not interested in me or my trophies. The boy's father responded sarcastically, 'What is the use of all these trophies? If the girl is beautiful, then husband is happy and the life is happy.'

My father, noticing the awkwardness of the situation, tried to take control. He turned toward the boy and politely asked him, 'Do you want to talk to Maya?'

Before the boy could answer, his mother intervened, 'There is no need for him to talk. He has left the decision on us.'

Knowing what the outcome would be my father stepped in to prevent me from being embarrassed any more.

'Betey Maya, why don't you go inside and help Sapna.' he said.

I got up and left, but although my parents thought I was out of earshot I hid in the corner in order to hear what the groom's parents thought about me, although, in my heart, I knew what their response would be.

Thinking I was out of sight, my father politely asked boy's parents, 'So what do you think we should do now? If you approve of our daughter, we can proceed further.'

Again, the boy's mother interjected, 'I like your daughter, but not Maya. I hope you don't mind, but in my family there have not been any dark skinned bride for generations. If you want we can consider my son's alliance with Sapna.'

'Thank you for being forthright, but we cannot marry our younger daughter before we marry Maya,' said my father, politely showing them the door.

After a few months, my family was again getting ready for another prospective groom's family visit. But this time my mom wanted to be more careful. She examined the room where the guests would be sitting. There was one spot where the window let in the most light. With the help of Sapna she rearranged the furniture so I would be seated in the most lit area so the sun light would add glow to my skin.

After helping Mom, Sapna came back to the kitchen to help me prepare snacks for the guests.

Mom did some more rearranging. She then came to the kitchen and whisked Sapna away to outside the kitchen. I was curious to know why Mom did that. I tiptoed near them and hid behind a door.

I saw my Mom whispering something into Sapna's ears. I could not clearly hear what she told her but I think she instructed her to not come in the living room in front of guests. I quickly tiptoed back to the kitchen.

The ritual started again – The guests came and as they sat down, my mother yelled into the kitchen asking me to bring some drinks into the living room. I walked into the room. The groom and his family all got their first look at me. As planned by my mother, I was seated on the designated seat.

The boy's mother was carefully watching my every move. As I got up to serve them tea, I had to move out of the sunlight, and the boy's mother got a glimpse of my exposed hands. There was suddenly a concerned look on her face. She signaled to her husband to pay attention to my bare hands.

The boy's father addressed my father – 'Mr. Prasad, how many children do you have?'

'We have two daughters. The other daughter is one year younger than Maya.' he replied.

'Where is your other daughter?' asked boy's father.

Before father could respond, my mother jumped in, 'Oh, she is visiting her grandmother.'

My father gave Mom a questioning look. Both my father and I knew why my Mom was hiding Sapna.

The boy's mother wanted to see more of me to find out how dark I was. She tried to get a little friendly with me.

'Oh come on Maya, we are very liberated family; you don't have to cover yourself up so much. Please remove your gown and be comfortable.' she told me.

My mother helplessly looked at the situation and quietly put on a fake smile.

Boy's mother helped me take out my gown. Now my dark hands were exposed.

The expression of boys's parents changed suddenly. Then my mother, in a desperate last attempt, broke the silence, 'Maya has always come first in her class. She has won numerous awards.'

Needless to say they had already made up their mind. They excused themselves and left.

I could see that my parents were very frustrated and disappointed. My mother did not want me to see the pain she was going through. She instructed me to go inside, and once again I knew I had been rejected because of my dark skin.

After I left the living room, I heard my mother speak to my father. 'Now the only way to get her married is to offer a big dowry. Please go tomorrow and find out how much money we can borrow,' she suggested.

'You worry unnecessarily," he said, "She is still very young. Let her finish her studies.'

'No, if she is old then there will be nobody who will accept her. I am convinced that she'll not find anybody unless we give a big dowry,' she cautioned.

As I heard all of this I could not contain the tears anymore. I cried for hours wondering why I was being punished. Had I done some deed in my past life, and was now paying my dues? I spent hours trying to discover why I was being tortured, but the answers never came.

Meanwhile Sapna walked in to comfort. She had something in her hand.

'Here you go Maya.'

'What is it?' I asked.

'Milk coffee, *Maa* wants you to drink it.'

CHAPTER XI

Restoring Bonds

"Then what happened?" asked Natasha.

Maya continued - "Well, this routine continued and nobody agreed to marry me. Then my father took out a big loan and started offering dowry to boys' parent. Then, one day God smiled on us and we were visited by your dad's family. Before they could say anything, my parents told them about the dowry that they were willing to give."

Natasha snapped back, "Wait, did *Pappa* take dowry from your family?"

Maya continued, "No, your dad would never do that. Your *Dadi Maa* (Om's mother) worked with Mahatma Gandhi during her youth. They were totally against even at a mention of dowry. I don't know what they saw in me, they all accepted me with no strings attached and no dowry."

"I know *Pappa*," said Natasha proudly, "He would never do anything like that."

"I've been so lucky to have married to your father," said Maya.

Both sat quietly for a few seconds. Then Natasha got up and hugged her mother.

"*Maa*, I'm sorry I snapped at you," Natasha apologized, "I was not in a good mood this morning."

"*Betey*, the only reason I do what I do is to make sure that you don't have to go through what I went through," said Maya.

"But *Maa*, the times have changed," explained Natasha, "People are not as conservative as they were in your time."

"That is exactly what I used to tell my mother," countered Maya, "I used to believe that during those days times had changed. People are judged by their quality, not by their color. I knew it then and I know it now, people have not changed, nor will they ever change."

"But *Maa*, you got a great husband, didn't you?" questioned Natasha.

"Yes, I did, and I know you'll also get a great husband," Maya responded with a smile, but while she was reassuring Natasha of her future, she wondered if her daughter would be as lucky as she was.

CHAPTER XII

Points Of Views

Natasha was sitting in her company's cafeteria having lunch with one of her girl friends, Shweta, who was very light skinned 22 year old girl and also a little on the heavy side.

"Hey Natasha, did you finish your presentation?" asked Shweta.

"No, I worked on it last night for several hours, but did not save it," said Natasha grudgingly, "In the morning there was a power outage, and I lost everything.

I'm going to work on it again tonight. I was such an idiot."

"Bummer," sympathised Shweta.

Meanwhile, the waiter came to take their order, "Madam, what can I get for you?"

"I'm very hungry; I'll take some chicken biriyani, raita and a black tea please," said Shweta.

"I'll just take the house salad and a glass of lime water," Natasha told the waiter.

"Natasha, what is going on? Are you dieting? These days' boys like a little meat on their women," she teased.

"No, if I eat a heavy lunch, I feel tired and sleepy," Natasha clarified.

Shweta was also surprised that Natasha was not drinking black tea. "You're not going to drink black tea?" asked Shweta, "I thought you liked black tea."

"Yes, I do like it, but *Maa* does not want me to drink it," said Natasha.

"Why?" Shweta followed up. "*Maa* thinks, that drinking black tea makes skin darker," said Natasha meekly.

"Natasha, do you honestly believe in this garbage?" asked Shweta. "No, I don't. But I'm doing it for her. And besides why take any chances," she defended.

"Why take a chance for what? Natasha, are you planning to continue the age old nonsensical beliefs?" Shweta pushed on.

Natasha tried to find a way out of this. "It's very hard to convince *Maa*," she explained, "She has grown up believing all this nonsense. If it gives *Maa* some satisfaction and brings piece to her mind I don't mind not drinking black tea. But sometimes I do cheat and drink when *Maa* is not around."

"Well, right now your mother is not here, so come on and drink a cup of black tea with me," suggested Shweta.

"OK fine," agreed Natasha, "I just hope *Maa* doesn't find out."

She turned towards the waiter, "Waiter, can you please bring me also a cup of black tea."

"Yes Maam", said the waiter.

After the waiter was gone, Shweta started another interesting topic. "How are the marriage proposals coming along?" she inquired smilingly.

"I don't really pay attention to that," replied Natasha, "All I know is that my pictures are being sent out like newspapers."

Shweta wondered why an educated and beautiful girl like her was subjecting herself to this. "Natasha, you're so beautiful, I'm sure if you allow and open up to boys there will be many guys who will die to marry you," she suggested.

"I don't know about that, but I've decided to let my parents make that decision," responded Natasha.

Shweta pushed on, "But why? This is 21st century. How can they decide what is best for you?"

Natasha defended her decision, "I disagree. When we choose a mate we are often not objective because we are blinded by love, lust, and infatuation. And moreover, I believe that during the courtship period, both partners try to put in front only their best foot, and thus, you don't get the whole picture."

Shweta squinted her eyes conveying her disagreement with Natasha's argument. "But you choose your own friends, don't you?" she asked.

"Yes, we do choose our friends," said Natasha emphatically, "But with friends, it's different. First of all, you choose friends based only on certain qualities of theirs. For example, you're my good friend because I like the intensity of intellectual discussions that you engage me, just like you're doing it right now. I like Rekha for her sensitivity about others. I like Rahul for his amazing sense of humor. But in a husband, you may want more than just certain qualities."

Shweta was still not convinced. She pressed on, "But what makes you so sure that your parents can find a match with the right qualities?"

"There is no guarantee; but considering that *Maa* and *Pappa* have more than 50 years of combined experience over me, the chances are that they will choose someone who will overall be good for me," answered Natasha.

"Overall good?" retorted Shweta with raised eyebrows.

Natasha smiled, "You don't know my parents. They will do a very thorough research on the prospective groom as well as on his family and friends. They will probably talk to his school teachers, professors, neighbors, employers, and anybody to find if he is hiding any skeletons in his closet."

Shweta appeared not to be convinced by her reasoning, but she still admired Natasha's total trust in her parents.

Shweta put on a very serious face and said, "Natasha, you're my good friend but I hate you."

"Hate me? Why?" wondered Natasha.

"Because you're such a model daughter; my parents love you more than they love me," Shweta griped.

Natasha laughed, "Thank you - and you know what? My *Maa* loves you a lot too. And among other qualities of yours she is a fan of your skin color."

Shweta laughed.

"Natasha, can I ask you a personal question?" Shweta asked again.

"More personal than what we have been talking so far?" Natasha quipped.

"Kind of"

Natasha wonderd what else was in her mind? She looked at her curiously, "OK, shoot."

Shweta adjusted herself in her chair as if to get ready to ask some very "heavy duty" question, "OK, here it is. You have told me a lot of stories about your *Maa* on how she wishes that you were white. How do you feel about it?"

Shweta continued to look at her waiting for her to say something. After a few moments, Natasha responded, "Let me clarify some things about my *Maa*. I know my mother has a complex about dark skin. But in defense of my mother, I know for sure that as a result of what she went through as a young girl she has a lot of compassion for dark skinned girls. Among all the maids that we have had, she has gone out of her way to help the darker skinned maids. In fact, she has even paid for all the educational expenses of one of my maid's daughter, Radha, who is a dark skinned girl. In fact Radha is almost like family to us."

Shweta followed up, "Would your mother have paid for her educational expenses if Radha was white?"

Natasha looked up to think, "I don't know for sure, but perhaps she would not have."

Shweta pried further, "Don't you think this extra compassion, and this extra kindness reminds the receiver that she is a lesser human being?"

Natasha pondered and slowly nodded her head in agreement, "Well you could be right. Her noble intentions may have negative consequences, and that is why I'm determined to not perpetuate this color discrimination and make sure that my children do not inherit this trait from my family."

Shweta continued to pry, "Let me ask you a hypothetical question. What if your daughter is dark skinned? How will you feel?"

Natasha was slightly uneasy with this question. But because of the hypothetical nature of the question, she did not take it personally. She paused to think for a good answer.

"All I would for my child is to be healthy, loving and smart," she answered.

"You did not answer my question," Shweta pressed on.

"Let me just say this - I want my children to inherit all the values of my parents except my *Maa*'s pity for dark skin," said Natasha.

Shweta could see that Natasha was not comfortable with this discussion. But at the same time she did not want to let her off the hook so easily. "Well I'm not going to push you anymore, but you still did not answer my question," she said.

Feeling cornered and unable to clearly answer Shweta's question, Natasha immediately fired back, "Let me ask you the same question."

Shweta looked at Natasha and asked, "How will I feel if I get a dark skinned daughter?"

"Yes."

Now Shweta felt cornered and speechless. She paused, gazed towards the ceiling, struggling for a response, "I don't know. I haven't thought about it."

"So think about it now like you asked me to do," said Natasha.

After a little thinking, Shweta found a way to give an indirect answer, "You know, the truth is that I'm fond of brown skin and green eyes. If my daughter has these two things, I'll be the happiest mom. But I know for sure that I'll never ever believe or be a part of any of the skin whitening rituals."

Natasha smiled and nodded her head. Both of them knew exactly what their uneasiness in answering that question meant. To lighten up the conversation, Shweta added, "Natasha, let me also tell you a secret. I'm always a sucker for dark skinned men. But your brother is an exception. I would fall for him anytime even though he is not a dark skinned."

As both of them burst into laughter, Natasha looked at her watch and realized that her lunch time was already over, "If this interview is over, can we leave now? We have already taken a long lunch break," she suggested with a smile.

Natasha started to collect her purse. But before she got up, Shweta asked, "Natasha, one more question."

Natasha looked at her inquisitively wondering what is left to ask.

"You said earlier that you pick friends based only on their certain qualities. You already said that you like my intellectual discussion ability. Are there any qualities of mine, which you're not a fan of?" asked Shweta.

Shweta looked at Natasha for her response. Natasha smiled quietly. There was no response from Natasha.

"Come on, I'm waiting," persisted Shweta.

"Waiting for what?"

"Just one quality of mine that you're not fond of."

"You really want to know?" asked Natasha.

"I'm all ears," said Shweta.

Natasha paused for a few moments, pondered on what to say. She then looked at her from head to feet, "I'm not too excited about your sense of color coordination."

Shweta quickly looked at her mismatched red shirt and pink pants and then responded excitedly, "I knew that. I knew that. And you know what? That is why I always want you to come to shopping with me."

They both laughed again.

"Let's go back," said Natasha, as she picked up her stuff and proceeded to her office.

After a few minutes, her computer rang because of an incoming video chat request. It was Vikram. His picture showed up on the computer monitor.

"*Bhaiyaa*, how are you?"

"I'm OK. Where are you right now?" asked Vikram.

"In my office," she answered.

"Is there anybody else in your office?" Vikram asked again.

"No… why?" she wondered.

"Listen, *Maa* and *Pappa*'s 25th marriage anniversary is on June 21," he said.

She immediately perked up, "Yes, I know. Are you planning to come?"

"Yes, that is why I'm calling you. But, don't tell *Maa* or *Pappa* that I'm coming. Let's surprise them."

Natasha was thrilled to learn that, "That's great. I don't know if I can hide my excitement, but it'll be really great. They will be so happy."

"You must keep it a total secret," he instructed, "You always thought acting was very easy, so this is your chance to show off your acting skills. We need to plan a great party for them, but they should not get any wind of it."

Natasha tried to control her excitement, "My lips are sealed."

"I've some ideas on what we can do. You also think about it. But the most important thing is that this should be a total surprise," said Vikram.

"Is it a secret for *Maa* and *Pappa* or for all the family and friends?" she asked.

"My idea was to only keep *Maa* and *Pappa* in the dark. We'll have to involve everybody else in this. What do you think?" Vikram asked.

"I think it's a great idea," she said excitedly, "It will be a lot of fun. I'm already excited. Let's hope nobody spills the beans."

"I think it'll work," he said, "Listen, I'll call Tullu *Chacha* (Vikram's uncle), *Dadi Maa* (Vikram's paternal grandmother) and *Maa*'s and *Pappa*'s friends. You just organize the actual party."

"So, you're going to tell *Maa* and *Pappa* that you're not coming?" she inquired.

"Yes, and this will be a test of my acting prowess too," he said, "Listen, I'm also planning one more thing for the party."

"What is that?"

"I think you and I should sing a song for *Maa* and *Pappa*," Vikram suggested.

"Which song?"

"I think we should write our own song, give it music and then perform," he proposed.

"Write our own song?" she asked nervously.

"Yes, write our own song," said Vikram, "In fact I already have some ideas. I'll email it to you soon. Meanwhile, practice your guitar and make sure it's properly tuned."

"I did not know that my brother is a poet too," she said with a laugh.

"Well, for all you know I could be the next Shakespere," he joked, "But, seriously, it's just a bunch of rhyming lines. OK sis, you must do a couple of things soon. First, reserve a good outdoor place for the party and select a good menu for the dinner. I'm dying for some good Indian food."

"Do you want me to include anything special in the menu?" she asked.

"Yes, please add *Baigan Ka Bharta* (mashed spiced roasted eggplant) and *Karhi* (a spicy yogurt concoction)."

"Done. Anything else?"

"Listen, I'll not call you at home. I'll be calling you at work at the same time everyday to discuss the progress," he said, "Also, when I tell *Maa* and *Pappa* that I'm not coming, please play along and show your sadness and disappointment. I'll call *Dadi Maa* and Tullu *Chacha* to get them also on board."

"OK"

"Sis, I've one more secret."

"Secret! What is it?"

Vikram was quite for a few moments. Natasha's curiosity was out of control, "What is it, brother?"

"Are you ready?" asked Vilkram.

"Come on, you're killing me," yammered Natasha.

Vikram whispered into the microphone, "I'm in love."

Natasha could not believe what she just heard. She almost screamed, "What!? Did you say you're in love?"

"Yes, that is what I said."

Natasha was already too excited with the thought of seeing her brother soon and how happy that would make her parents. The news of her brother being in love added to her euphoria. She wanted to know everything about the girl, "Who is she? Is she Indian or American?"

"She is American," replied Vikram.

"Oh my God! Do you have her picture?"

"Yeah, I'll email that to you."

She could not wait to see her picture. "Email it to me right now!" she pleaded.

"Ok," he said.

"What is her name?" she asked.

"Megan"

"Check your email. I just sent you her picture."

Natasha quickly checked her email and opened her picture.

Natasha's voice was shaking with excitement. She quickly opened Megan's picture, "Oh, she is so pretty."

Natasha continued to admire Megan's picture for a few moments. "But she doesn't look white," she asked.

"Yes, she isn't white," he replied.

"Are you planning to marry her?" she asked.

"Yes, that is my plan."

"When are you getting married? Wait, what about mom and… "

Vikram cut her off, "I know. You don't have to say it again. I've worried about it enough."

They both were quite for a few moments. Natasha broke the silence, "I've an idea."

Vikram was in a desparate need of some help here, "Oh, please tell me. I need help."

"Why don't you bring her along with you for the anniversary party?" she proposed.

Vikram was not too thrilled with this idea, "Are you out of your mind? Once *Maa* finds out about her, it'll spoil the entire party."

Natasha pondered some more, "You know what? Let's do this. You bring her to India. She'll come to the party as the new girl from my office. And then after the party when the dust settles we'll try to feel out *Maa* and *Pappa* about her. But you'll have to train Megan to play along."

Vikram was not sure about this plan, "Natasha, are you sure this is the right way to approach this?"

"Don't worry about it *Bhaiyya*. We'll find a way out. And besides, I'm dying to meet her."

"OK Natasha, make sure to keep this a secret. I'll call you tomorrow at the same time. See ya."

"Bye."

Natasha clinched her fist in excitement and anticipation.

CHAPTER XIII

Remote Planning

Dr. Radha Kumar, the daughter of the maid servant Kamla who worked at Srivastava's house grew up to be a beautiful dark skinned young woman. She worked as a gynecologist in a local hospital. Vikram always considered her his best friend and a mentor.

Radha had just walked into her office and sat at her desk when her phone rang.

"Dr. Radha Kumar," said Radha as she answered.

"Dr. Radha Kumar, can I speak to Dr. Katori Kumar."

Radha got really excited. She knew that there were only two people in this world who called her "Katori" – her dad and Vikram. It must be Vikram. She almost screamed - "Oh Vickie, how are you?"

"I'm doing well Katori. How are you?"

"I'm fantastic. When are you coming to India?"

"In two weeks."

Radha was ecstatic when she heard that. She screamed, "Two weeks!! That is super. So you're going to be here for *Mem Sahib's* anniversary."

"Yes," said Vikram.

"Oh, *Mem Sahib* and *Maalik* will be so happy," she said.

In spite of becoming a very successful doctor, Radha still addressed Vikram's parents as *Mem Sahib* and *Maalik,* as if she was still their maid servant.

Vikram shared his surprise party plan with her, "Katori, but this is all top secret. *Maa* and *Pappa* must not know about it. We are planning a surprise party."

"A surprise party! That is even better."

"Katori, but you have to help me out," said Vikram.

"Tell me what I've to do?" she asked.

Vikram described his plan – "First you call Natasha and help her organize the party. But remember it is all top secret. And the second thing is that I'm planning to sing a song for *Maa* and *Pappa*, and I've already talked to Natasha, I want you to also sing and play keyboard."

"Vickie, I think just you and Natasha should sing," suggested Radha, "You're *Mem Sahib's* children."

Vikram knew that he could make her agree, "Katori, if you ever say this again, I'll never speak with you again. If you don't sing with us, then the whole party is off."

The threat worked and Radha relented immediately, "Ok Babba, I'm sorry. I'll play keyboard and also sing with you and, but which song?"

"I'll let you know soon. And there is one more thing."

"What is it?" Radha wondered.

Vikram whispered into the computer's microphone, "I think I'm in love."

Radha screamed with excitement, "What? You're in love? Who is she? Have you decided to marry her?"

"Calm down, calm down. Yes, I want to marry her but only if you, Natasha, *Maa* and *Pappa* agree to that," said Vikram.

Radha was so excited that she couldn't breathe.

"Can you email me her picture?" she asked excitedly.

"Ok. I'll do it right now."

Vikram emailed Megan's picture to Radha. After a few moments, Radha's computer beeped indicating the arrival of a new email. She quickly opened it and looked at Megan's picture.

"Oh, Vickie she is so beautiful. Where is she from?"

"She is American," he answered.

"But she doesn't look white," she asked.

"Yes, because she is not white, and it's not just whites who inhabit the US," gibed Vikram.

"Is she coming with you?" she asked.

"That is the plan. Please check with Natasha to see how we are going to break the ice to *Maa* and *Pappa*."

"Oh my God, it's going to be so much fun. I can't wait," said Radha excitedly.

"Katori, I've to run now. I've to do many things before I come there. I'll talk to you to plan all this," he said, "OK, bye, and don't forget to call Natasha."

"I won't. Bye Vickie."

Vikram took his cellphone out and called his uncle Atul (Om's younger brother). He always referred to his uncle as Tullu *Chacha*.

"Tullu *Chacha*, *Namstey*, this is Vikram."

"Oh, Vikram, how are you?" said Atul excitedly, "Are you calling from the US?"

Atul's wife, Mukta, ran to other phone to talk to Vikram.

"Yes, I'm in the US."

"Hey Vikram *beta*, how are you?" said Mukta from another phone.

"*Chachi* (aunt), I am good. How are you?"

"I am also good. When are you coming to India?"

"That is why I'm calling you. Natasha and I are planning a surprise 25th anniversary party for *Maa* and *Pappa* on June 21," told Vikram

"A surprise party?" Both Tullu and Mukta spoke at the same time.

"Do *Bhaiya* (Om) and *Bhabhi* (Maya) know about it?" wondered Atul.

"Oh, come on Atul, if *Bhaiyya* and *Bhabhi* knew, then how it'll be a surprise party?" chaffed Mukta.

Tullu realized his buffoonery, "Oh, of course, of course. So what is the plan?"

"The plan is that we are going to have a big party. Natasha will reserve Gymkhana country club hall for the party. She and I are also planning to sing a song for *Maa* and *Pappa*," explained Vikram.

Mukta loved the plan, "That is great."

"I need help from both of you. I want *chacha* to play Tabla and *chachi* you'll help direct the musical part," instructed Vikram.

"Play tabla? I haven't played in years."

"You guys have 2 weeks to practice. You have to do it," demanded Vikram.

"Which song are you going to sing?" asked Mukta.

"I've written my own song."

Tullu was happily surprised to hear that, "You have written your own song? That is wonderful. I didn't know that we had a poet in our family."

"But how are we going to practice?" wondered Mukta.

"Don't worry; we have a computer expert in our family. Natasha will set everything up and we'll practice it over the internet via computers," said Vikram.

Not being too familiar with the Internet, Tullu was not too sure how it was going to work out, "How can you do it on a computer?"

Vikram allayed his concerns, "You leave this to Natasha and me. She'll set up the whole thing."

"That will be interesting. Who else is playing what?" asked Mukta.

"I'll play the lead guitar; Natasha will play the base guitar, Katori will play keyboard and *Dadi Maa* will play *dholak*, and that is it," he explained.

"That sound's great. So Vickie, when are we going to have our first rehearsal?" wondered Tullu.

"Do you have time the day after tomorrow during the lunch?" asked Vikram.

"Practice during lunch? Why?" asked Mukta.

"We can practice only during the lunch time otherwise *Maa* and *Pappa* will get the wind of it. Also, Natasha can come to your house directly from her work and set up the internet so we can practice. Remember, we have to keep the whole thing very secret," Vikram clarified.

Mukta was already set to go, "OK, let's start the practice from tomorrow. I am so excited."

"Tullu *chacha* and *chachi ji*, I'll have to go. I'll talk to you tomorrow."

* * *

Vikram's grandmother lived in a small apartment in an *ashram*. Mahatma Ghandhi had a strong influence on her. She worked with him during the Indian independence struggle when she was just a teenager. Since she retired, she dedicated her life to public service. She spent most of her time in praying, gardening, and stitching clothes for homeless.

She was working on her sewing machine stitching blouses when suddenly the doorbell rang.

"Come in, the door is open," she said.

A middle aged man entered the door and greeted her, "*Namastey Maa Ji*!"

She looked at her through her glasses, "Oh Jagdish, I was just thinking about you. How are things at the Women Rehabilitation Center?" she asked.

"All the girls at the center are very thankful to you for providing them clothes to wear," he said smilingly.

"I am thankful to them. Because of these girls I've some purpose in life," she said.

She put blouses in a large plastic bag and handed it over to him, "Please take these and give to the girls."

He took the bags, bent down to show his respect to her., "Namastey *Maa Ji*. I'll leave now."

"Namastey, I'll call you when I've more clothes ready," she said.

"Very well *Maa ji*!"

After he left, she went back to stitching. After a few minutes, her phone rang.

It was Vikram at the other end, "*Dadi Maa*," said Vikram.

"Oh Vickie, how are you *beta*?" she said excitedly.

"I'm well, *Dadi Maa*."

"*Beta*, I think about you all the time," she said.

"*Dadi Maa*, that is why I'm coming to India."

She was very excited to hear that, "Oh really! When?"

"*Dadi Maa* we are all planning to give a surprise anniversary party to *Maa* and *Pappa* on June 21," he said.

"So Om and Maya don't know that you're coming?" she wondered.

"Yes, *Dadi Maa*. They don't know that. So please keep it a top secret," instructed Vikram.

"I'll try to put on a poker face when I talk to them," she chuckled.

"There is one more thing *Dadi Maa*," he continued.

"What is it?"

"Natasha, Katori and I are planning to sing in the party. I want you to play your *dholak*," he said.

"Sure, I'll love to play *dholak*. But when exactly are you coming and where will you stay if you are going to keep it a secret?" she wondered.

"I was planning to stay with you," he said.

She was ecstatic to learn that, "Really? I'll cook all your favorite dishes. When are you coming?"

"I'll arrive there in about two weeks," he said.

"*Beta*, please come a little early. Spend some more time with your *Dadi Maa*," she pleaded.

"*Dadi Maa*, I wanted to do that but I'm not getting enough time off from my job."

"I understand. Do whatever you have to do. I am anxiously waiting to spend time with you. It'll be just you and me," she said.

"I'm looking forward to it too *Dadi Maa*, he said, "One more thing though *Dadi Maa* - Natasha will explain to you how we are going to practice the song."

"OK *Beta*."

"*Dadi Maa* I've to go now. I'll talk to you during our practice session. Natasha will tell you everything. Remember, *Maa* and *Pappa* should not get any wind of what we are doing," Vikram explained.

She reassured him, "Don't worry, nobody will know."

"OK, bye *Dadi Maa*."

"God bless you, *beta*."

CHAPTER XIV

A Cover Up

It was night time at the Srivastava's house. Maya and Natasha were working in the kitchen and Om was washing the dishes in the sink when the phone started ringing.

Natasha ran to the phone. It was Vikram calling.

"Hi *Bhaiyya*"

"Hi, sis, what is going on?" Vikram asked.

Natasha looked around and whispered into the phone, "*Maa* and *Pappa* are in Kitchen. We are getting dinner ready. They have no clue about our plans. I'm so excited."

Vikram whispered into the phone, "I've already talked to Tullu *chacha*, *Dadi Maa* and Katori. Let's not talk about it here. We'll talk about it at your work."

Meanwhile, Maya called from kitchen, "Natasha, who is on the phone?"

"It's *Bhaiyya*."

She immediately turned toward the computer microphone and whispered, "*Bhaiyya*, *Maa* and *Pappa* are coming. Be careful."

"OK"

Maya and Om came running to the phone.

"*Beta* Vickie, are you going to be able to come here in a couple of weeks?" asked Maya.

Vikram tried his acting skills and pretended as if he did not know what his mother was talking about, "What is going on in a couple of weeks?" he asked.

Maya was a little disappointed that he did not remember his parents' marriage anniversary but she tried to not show her disappointment, "Nothing is going on. I just wanted to see you," she answered. Standing right behind her mother, Natasha tried to hide her smile.

Vikram knew that his mother was disappointed but he must continue his act to make his plan succeed, "*Maa*, I want to come there but it has been really hectic here. I may be able to get some time off after about six months."

Maya was even more disheartened. "Six months?" she said disappointingly.

Vikram felt uncomfortable causing emotional pain to his mother. He tried to comfort her without disclosing anything, "*Maa*, I'll try to make it earlier, but next month seems almost impossible."

She felt helpless, "What can I say *beta*? This is the price we have to pay for letting you go abroad."

"Oh *Maa*, don't be disappointed. I'll see you sooner than you think," he comforted her.

Maya knew that he was saying this just to make her feel better.

"Is *Pappa* around?" asked Vikram.

"Yes, he is right here."

"Son, how is your work going?" asked Om.

"Hi *Pappa*, It's going very good."

Om was not as disappointed as Maya because he believed that Vikram's top priority should be his career.

"Did you get the Microsoft contract?" asked Om.

"We are still working on it, but it's looking really good," answered Vikram.

"It'll be good for your career if you get that," said Om.

"I know *Pappa*, we are trying our best."

"How is your health? Are you exercising every day?" asked Om.

"Not every day, but I go to gym whenever I get a chance," he replied, "How is your blood pressure?"

"Well your mom is basically starving me so I guess my blood pressure is good."

Maya jumped in, "*Beta*, don't believe anything he says. Just yesterday, he ate two *samosas*."

"*Maa*, let *Pappa* indulge once in a while," said Vikram.

"He indulges much more than once in a while," complained Maya.

"Is Natasha around?" asked Vikram.

"I'm right here," said Natasha.

"Sis, how are you?" asked Vikram.

Natasha tried to put on a sad face, "I'm disappointed that you're not coming."

Vikram interrupted her, "I know, I know. But I'm kinda busy planning a big event."

Om came to the defense of Vikram, "Don't worry too much about coming here. Your career is the top priority right now. We can wait."

Dejected, Maya tried to accept the situation, "*Beta*, I know you are working very hard. Pay attention to your health."

Vikram tried to lighten her up, "*Maa*, don't worry about my health. I was 160 pounds when I came here, and now I am 165 pounds. I think for a 5 feet 11 inches man, this is slighty overweight."

"No, don't worry, you will not get overweight. There are no fat genes in our family," said Maya.

Vikram was having hard time playing out this act. Before he let the cat out of the bag, he concluded the conversation, "Ok, guys, I've to go to work now, and I'll talk to you later," Vikram said as he hung up.

"I cannot believe that Vickie did not remember our marriage anniversary, and that too 25th," Maya stammered, "He used to be the first one who would remind us of all our birthdays, anniversary dates, - and not just ours - all his uncles, and aunts, and friends." She waited for the phone to ring and Vikram to acknowledge his mistake, but it never did.

Om was more pragmatic about this. He could relate to Vikram being very busy in his work and thus was prone to forget things. Om recalled many of his own forgetfulnesses. But, he knew that Maya thought differently. He tried to mitigate Maya's anxiety.

"Perhaps he has too many things in his mind," he defended Vikram, "I am sure he will remember it soon and call you."

Maya put her own spin to it, "I am sure that is what happened. The poor guy is working too hard. I wish he could come here soon so I can marry him to some nice girl so that he does not have to run around every day for food."

Natasha taunted her mother, "So that is the purpose of a wife – to cook food for her husband so he doesn't have to run around?"

"You guys love to stretch and distort everything I say," complained Maya.

Om broke in their argument, "OK guys, I am hungry. Let's get dinner ready."

CHAPTER XV

Tune The Guitar

Vikram was at the other end of phone, "Hey Sis, can you set our first music practice session tomorrow at lunch at Tullu *Chacha*'s home?"

"I guess, I can; but I'll need my guitar. How will I get the guitar from our house because normally I leave before *Maa*. She'll wonder why I'm taking my guitar to office."

"Sis, this is an easy problem. I'm sure you can solve it. I'll email you the lyrics of the song in a few minutes. I'll call you tomorrow at exactly 12 O'Clock Indian time."

"I'll get everything ready. And you know what?"

"What?"

"*Maa* was very disappointed yesterday," she said.

"Disappointed because I'm not coming?" he asked.

"That and you did not remember her 25 marriage anniversary," she said.

"Yeah, she seemed kinda disappointed. I was having a hard time acting that part out. But let's try to keep it that way. It'll all be worth it when they see the surprise party."

"OK, I'll talk to you later," she said.

"OK Sis, I'll talk to you tomorrow at noon. Bye."

"See ya."

Natasha went to her office and called Tullu *Chacha* and *Dadi Maa* to set the music practice meeting at Tullu's house at noon. Then she called Radha, "Hey Radha, this is Natasha."

Radha was expecting her call, "Hi Natasha, how are you?"

"You already know what *Bhaiyya* is planning," said Natasha.

"Yes, we had a long chat on that," said Radha, "Actually I'm quite excited."

"Me too; I hope everything goes smoothly," said Natasha.

"Well just tell me what I've to do to make it happen," said Radha.

"I think you and I should get together for lunch and start planning the whole thing," Natasha proposed.

Radha agreed, "Sure."

"But before that we have to do one more thing," said Natasha, "*Bhaiyya* wants to do the first music practice session tomorrow. He wants all of us to come to Tullu *Chacha*'s house during lunch. Can you come?"

Radha already knew about the music practice, "I'll definitely come. I'll ask some other doctor to cover my patients during lunch."

Simultaneously, Natasha was also wondering how she was going to get her guitar from her home without her parents knowing about it. She quickly conceived of a plan. She shared the plan with Radha. "One more thing, Radha," said Natasha.

"What is it?" asked Radha.

Natasha explained her plan, "I need my guitar for this practice but I don't want *Maa* or *Pappa* to know about it. So the plan is that you call *Maa* and tell her that Sachin (Radha's husband) wants to buy a new guitar and he wanted to see a good quality guitar to see how it feels. And that you want to borrow my guitar for a couple of days."

"Hmm, that's a good idea," laughed Radha, "I think after all this is over we all could easily act in Bollywood."

"Haha, that would be nice," Natasha chuckled, "And remember - call at a time when I'm not there. So you'll have to tell the guitar story to *Maa*."

"So what will be the best time to call?" asked Radha.

Natasha pondered for a moment, "OK, let's do this. You call at my house exactly at 6:00 in the evening. I'll make sure that I lock myself in the bathroom at 6:00."

Radha chuckled again, "OK. Don't mess up."

"Oh believe me I won't. OK, so remember to call and I'll see you tomorrow."

"OK, bye"

"See ya"

* * *

Natasha entered her house. Maya was already there in the kitchen. Natasha looked at the clock. It was 5:50.

"*Maa*, where are you," she called.

"I am in the kitchen," answered Maya, "Come here and have some snacks."

Natasha put her bag down and ran to the kitchen. She started to munch on the stuff her mother was cooking, but while she was enjoying the snacks she realized that it was 6:00. She started to run to the bathroom. Then suddenly the phone rang.

Maya could not answer the phone because she was frying snacks. "*Betey* Natasha, can you please get the phone?" she said.

Natasha knew it must be Radha on the phone, "No *Maa*, I've to go the bathroom really bad."

"Get me the phone and then go," Maya said.

"No *Maa*, I've to go right now," said Natasha while running to bathroom.

Maya turned off the oven and rushed to receive the phone. Natasha locked herself in bathroom and stood close to door to listen to the conversation.

"Hello, *Mem Sahib*," greeted Radha.

Maya was always happy to talk to Radha. She was like her second daughter, "Oh Radha *betey*. You don't call me as much since you have become a doctor. And also, please stop calling me *Mem Sahib*."

"I've addressed you by this name since my childhood. I cannot change it now," said Radha.

"How is your husband?" asked Maya.

"He is good. How are Om *Sahib* and Natasha?"

"They are all fine."

"And how is Vickie," asked Radha.

Maya took a deep breath, "He is very busy. I was hoping that he will come for our 25th anniversary but he says that he cannot get the leave from work. Why don't you talk to him? He listens to you."

Radha obviously did not reveal anything about Vikram's plan, "OK I'll call him and try to twist his arm. I also needed to talk to Natasha."

Maya called for Natasha, "Natasha, Radha is on phone."

Natasha immediately opened the tap water pretending to not hear her. "Radha, Natasha is in bathroom. Do you want to leave her any message?" asked Maya.

Now here came Radha's first acting test. She already had everything written down what she was going to say. She started reading from her script, "Sachin (Radha's husband) is planning to learn the guitar. I told him that before he buys a guitar, he should try to play Natasha's guitar and get a few lessons from her."

"Yes, that is good idea. I'll get to see you guys more often," said Maya happily.

"*Mem Sahib*, I was hoping that Sachin can practice the guitar at our home before getting lessons from Natasha," clarified Radha.

"That is not a problem," Maya said, "I'll ask Natasha to take the guitar with her tomorrow to work. You can take it from her."

Radha clinched her fists in triumph, "Thank you, *Mem Sahib*. Why don't you come to our house someday?"

"Yes, sure *beta*. It has been several weeks since I saw you and Sachin. I'll see when Om is free and then I'll call you."

"Who was it *Maa*?" asked Natasha, timing her exit just as the phone conversation ended.

"It was Radha."

To put a little more realism into her act she asked, "Why didn't you call me? I wanted to talk to her."

"I called you, but you did not hear me. But you are going to see her tomorrow," said Maya.

Natasha tried to keep a straight face, "Why?"

"She wants your guitar. Sachin wants to learn guitar from you," said Maya.

Natasha showed her excitement, "Oh that is great. But I didn't know Sachin was interested in the guitar," said Natasha trying to hide her smile.

"Don't forget to take your guitar tomorrow with you. Radha will pick it up from your office," said Maya.

CHAPTER XVI

The Music Is Ready

It was the first day of music practice. Natasha had already set up the computer network where they all could practice with Vikram. Tullu, his wife, Natasha and her grandmother, and Radha waited with their musical instruments in front of a computer.

The computer beeped.

"Hi Bhaiyya" Natasha greeted.

"Hi everybody" Vikram greeted everybody.

"Are we all ready?" asked Vikram.

"Yes we are ready. I got the lyrics," answered Tullu.

Tullu and grand mother were quite excited at this whole setup. They were very impressed at Natasha's technical ability to make this happen.

"What do you think of the lyrics?" asked Vikram.

"Tell me the truth. Did you write it yourself or you stole it from somewhere?" asked Tullu.

"That means you liked the lyrics," answered Vikram.

"Liked it? I loved it. In fact I've already thought of music for that," said Tullu.

"That is great. Why don't you sing it" asked Vikram.

Tullu sang the first few lines while others joined in with their instruments. Vikram experimented with different tunes on his guitar. His plan was working.

CHAPTER XVII

Unconditional Love

Vikram wrapped up his work in his office in Philadelphia. He had not yet told Megan about his plans for India and that it involved her too. He needed to educate her about his mother's sensitivities. Also, he needed to convince her to be part of the act. He called Megan. She answered in a romantic voice, "Hello"

"What would it take to spend this evening with you?" he asked.

Megan was anxious to see Vikram. She pretended to think, "Hmmm… let me think. How about dinner at Olive Garden?"

"Oh, you read my mind. I was hoping that you would say that. So I'll pick you up at 6:30?" he said.

"I'll be ready."

* * *

Vikram and Megan sat in the restaurant. Both of them had a wine glass in front of them. He was looking for the right opportunity to explain his plans to her. What if she decided not to go along with the plan? What if she could not relate to his mother's bias against dark skin? What if his mother completely flipped out once she learned about his love affair with Megan? How would Megan feel? While he was processing these thoughts in his mind, Megan broke the silence – "Why are you so quiet? Is everything OK?" she asked.

He chose to explain everything to Megan without sugar coating it. He trusted her and believed that she would understand. He extended his hands and gently put it over Megan's hands, "Megan, do you trust me?"

She was slightly puzzled. She knew there was something in Vikram's mind.

"Why do you ask that?" she asked.

"Answer the question first," he insisted.

"Yes, I do trust you," she assured him.

"Completely?" he asked again.

"Yes, completely," she said smilingly.

He took a deep breath, "Well then I'm not going to mince any words and tell you without worrying about how to say it properly."

He paused for a second while she looked at him curiously. He was still thinking how to say what he wanted to say. She was anxious to hear him, "Vikram, please blurt it out. You're starting to worry me."

He looked into her eyes, bent forward with his hands still on top of her hands – "First, I want you to know that I want to grow old with you and I want you to be the person whose face I see the first when I wake up and whose face I see last before I go to bed."

She smiled.

He now looked at her expecting an answer from her, "So, how are you going to respond to this?"

"Ok, I like your style. Let me say without worrying about how to say it properly," she said.

She paused for a second. His hands were still on top of her hands. She sandwiched his hands between her hands tightened her grip as if not to let go of him. She paused. Vikram was anxious to hear her - "Come on, blurt it out. Your silence is killing me," he said.

Megan smiled shyly, "I'm going to to sound like an Indian girl, but here it goes - If I ever had children I want them to call you Dad, or would you prefer *Pappa*?"

Vikram was overcome by emotions. He knew that Megan was the girl of his dreams. He would fight any obstacle that came between her and him. He put his other hand on top of hers and clinched tightly. "I don't know what love is, but if love is longing to be with you all the time, then I'm in love with you," he affirmed.

She was glowing with happiness. She didn't want this conversation to end.

"Now that will be difficult to beat. But let me try anyway," she said.

She collected her thoughts for a second - "If love is laughing at your jokes, and always asking questions like 'Will Vikram like that?' or 'What would Vikram think about that?', then I know I'm in love with you."

"Megan, I hope I can live up to your expectations," he said emotionally.

"My only expectation from you is to just try to be 'you'," she said, "I like the way you are."

Vikram had yet to talk about his India trip. Now he felt more confident that Megan would support him. He took a sip from his wine glass.

"OK, so now that we have established that we both cannot live without each other, let's talk about some bumps that we have to overcome," he said.

"What bumps?" she wondered.

He explained, "You know my family is educated but my mother still clings to old conservative Indian values. And one of the dreams that she has been nursing ever since the day I was born is that she wants to be the one to choose a wife for me. So there will be some work on our part to convince her that you're her dream daughter-in-law."

She listened to him intently.

"So, what do I've to do?" she asked.

He continued, "Well the plan is that I want you to come with me to India. My parents don't know that I'm coming or you're coming. I want to give them a surprise on their 25th marriage anniversary. My sister Natasha, my grandmother and some other of my relatives are all part of the plan."

"So how do I fit in this plan?" she asked.

"You have the main role. Let me explain," he continued, "I'm still working on the exact script for you, but my general plan is that you'll be introduced to my parents as a colleague of my sister. You'll join us for the party and we'll try to create a situation where she gets to know you a little better. And once she knows you, there is no way that she will also not fall in love with you."

Megan was not too sure about this plan, "I don't know if I can pull it off."

Vikram was familiar with Megan's culture. He knew that she may not be able to relate to it. She may wonder why he can't tell his parents directly what was going on. She may think that he is a coward, and that he can't stand up to his parents. Before Megan said anything, he clarified, "Megan, if by any reasons you feel uncomfortable playing along, we'll drop this whole thing, and I'll just tell my parents that you're the girl of my dreams. Hopefully they will respect my decision, but if they don't, it's too bad. In fact I've already told about our relationship to my sister, my grandmother and my good friend Katori."

She understood his state of mind. In fact she knew about the Indian culture much more than what he expected.

"Since I've known you I've been reading books on Indian culture, and I've learnt a great deal on relationships in Indian family," she revealed, "If I've to change to respect cultural sensitivities, I'll gladly do it."

He was now more relaxed because she seemed to be agreeing to be part of the plan.

Megan, please don't change yourself. Perfection should be left untouched," he joked.

Megan smiled, "Perfection and me? You've had a bit too much to drink."

Vikram reciprocated with a smile.

"And, are you ready for another surprise?" she asked smilingly.

Vikram looked at her curiously, "What is it?"

"I've been learning Hindi too," she revealed.

Vikram was happily surprised, "Really? Say something in Hindi."

Megan spoke Hindi in her American accent, "*Apna haath idhar do* (Give me your hand)."

Vikram smiled with amazement and extended his hands toward her. Megan held Vikram's hand and again spoke in Hindi, "*Main jab jaagoon to tum mere samney ho, jab mai souun to tum mere sapney main ho* (when I'm awake, I long for you to be in front of me; when I sleep I long for you to be in my dreams)."

And as the clock struck 8 there they both sat. They gazed at each other with passion beyond belief, and they knew they would be happy together – forever hand in hand.

CHAPTER XVIII

A Web Of Lies

Om was in his office at his university. He had just finished talking on telephone to one of his acquaintances, Mr. Mathur, about the possibility of an arranged marriage between Mr. Mathur's son and Natasha. An arranged marriage process starts by each family exchanging the photographs of their marriageable son or daughter. Needless to say parents only send the best photographs. After this initial screening comes an elaborate research by each family on the other to make sure that each family is getting a "good deal." Once each side of the family (boy's family and girl's family) is satisfied with their research, they go to the next step, that is, face-to-face meeting between each family and an opportunity for the boy and girl to see and talk to each other. It's only after this final test that the arranged marriages consummate.

Om had already done the initial background research on Mr. Mathur's son. Based on his research, he established that Mr. Mathur's son would be an ideal groom for his daughter. It was now the time for the next step, which is a face-to-face meeting between the two families.

Om called Maya in her office.

"Maya, I've some very good news," said Om.

"What is it?" she asked.

"Looks like, the Mathurs liked Natasha's picture and they want to come to our house tomorrow with their son," he said.

Maya was thrilled to learn that. "Really?" she said excitedly.

"Yes, I talked to them and he sounded quite upbeat," he said, "On your way back please pick up some desert and snacks."

Then immediately Maya was worried because she knew that the pictures that she sent to Mathurs were the doctored pictures to hide Natasha's skin color. She knew that when they saw Natasha, they would find out the truth. She knew that two other families had rejected Natasha based on her skin color, and the Mathurs could be next.

"You don't sound very happy," wondered Om.

Maya tried to hide her concerns, "I am happy."

Om knew exactly what she must be thinking about. He knew that Maya must be worried because she doctored Natasha's image. Maya did not know that Om knew anything about it or that he sent the undoctored pictures to Mathurs.

"OK, I'll see you in the evening," he said.

Maya opened her computer and brought Natasha's real and doctored images on split screen. The left half of the screen showed a dark skinned Natasha and the right half of the screen shows doctored white skinned image. She murmured to herslf, "Why did I fix her pictures? They will now find out the truth about Natasha's dark skin."

Maya closed her eyes folded her hands in prayer and again murmured to herself, "Oh God, please save me."

While she was churning these thoughts, she conceived of another plan to cover up her doctoring episode. The only way out of this was to somehow hide Natasha's skin color yet again. She decided to hire a professional beautician to literally paint Natasha white. She knew one beautician, Rucksana, who had done Natasha's make up in the past. She called her beauty salon.

The phone rang in the salon. A woman answered the phone, "Good Morning. This is Star Salon. Where can I direct your call?"

"Can I speak to Rucksana?"

"Just a second" said the woman.

"Hello, this is Rucksana."

"Rucksana, this is Maya Srivastava."

"Hi, how are you Mrs. Srivastava?" said Rucksana.

"I am fine, thank you.Will you have time to do the make up of my daughter tomorrow around 5:00 pm?" asked Maya.

Rucksana checked her appointment schedule, "Looks like I've nothing scheduled for tomorrow at 5:00. So I'll come by your house."

"That is great. And listen, a boy's family is going to come to see Natasha, so I would like some skin foundation work done on her."

Rucksana had done many such "skin painting" jobs on other dark skinned girls including Natasha before. She knew exactly what Maya wanted.

"I've done it several time before on Natasha. I know exactly what needs to be done," she said.

"Ok then I'll see you tomorrow at 5:00," said Maya.

Maya could not concentrate on her work. She packed up her belongings and decided to go home. Her state of mind was like that of a thief who was afraid being caught. She was afraid that her cover up plan would be exposed. When she walked outside she felt as if everybody was watching her. She tried not to make an eye contact with anyone. She was not able to think rationally. She justified her actions as a mother's love for her daughter. Her responsibility was to make sure her children get the best in life, by hook or by crook.

She waited outside for a taxi on a busy intersection with high rise buildings all around. She waved for a taxi to stop. Many taxis drove by but none stopped. It was a busy time of the day.

Behind her at a distance there was a middle aged man standing in a corner quietly pulling hair from his nose. He grabbed one hair and started to pull on it while grimacing by tightening his eyes and face. Once the hair was out, he proudly held the hair with his fingers and looked at the hair as if telling the hair – "you can run but you can't hide." At that moment, one taxi stopped in front of Maya.

"Will you go to Bandaria Baag?" she asked.

"Yes Maam"

As soon as Maya started to board the taxi, the old man let out a big sneeze. Maya heard the sneeze and immediately pulled out of the auto rickshaw. (Most Indians believe that if somebody sneezes right before they are about to do something important – it's a bad omen. They believe that waiting for a few minutes right after the sneeze dispels the bad omen). The taxi driver looked back and wondered why she was not boarding.

She mumbled, "I got good news today and this stupid man had to sneeze right before I am about to leave."

Now she had to wait to let the bad omen pass. Seeing that taxi driver was in a hurry to move, she signaled the driver to go. The driver gave her bewildered look and sped off.

Maya looked at the man still pulling hair from his nose. In an attempt to try to get away from the old man, she started to walk. At the same time, the old man let loose another big sneeze. Maya closed her eyes and clinched her fist in disgust and froze. She continued to stand there for a few seconds to again let the bad omen pass. The old man was still busy pulling hair from his nose. She was afraid that the man was going to continue sneezing. She walked away rapidly before the man sneezed again. Maya moved to another intersection where she could not see or hear the old man. She waved for taxis again. She was concerned about the turn of events. The sneezing episode may have cast a spell on her daughter's chances of finding a good husband. Thus, she had to be extra careful to not do anything that was considered a bad omen.

After some time a taxi stopped in front of her. "Will you go to Bandaria Baag?" she asked.

"Yes Maam"

She boarded the taxi and it headed off to Bandaria Baag. When the taxi approached the Bandaria Baag neighborhood, Maya instructed the driver to stop near the vegetable market. She needed to purchase some vegetables and snacks for the upcoming visit with a potential groom for her daughter.

Once the taxi stopped and the driver was paid, Maya headed off to the vegetable market. After the purchase, Maya walked to her house. Natasha's scooter was already parked there.

"Natasha, are you home?" she called.

Natasha replied from her room, "Yes I'm here."

"Come to the kitchen, I'll make some milk coffee for you," said Maya.

"I'll be right there," Natasha responded.

Like her everyday ritual, Maya grated the white part of a coconut and mixed it with cashews in a bowl for Natasha. She was going on for a very important display tomorrow. Maya wanted to give Natasha whatever she could that had a potential of making any difference in her skin color.

Natasha walked into the kitchen and looked at all the bags of stuff that Maya brought. She opened the plastic bags one-by-one and started to munch on munchies that Maya had brought.

"Oh *Maa*, you brought so much of snacks. Is somebody coming to our house?" Natasha wondered.

"Yes," said Maya.

"Who?" asked Natasha.

Maya gave Natasha the bowl of grated white of coconut and cashews, "Stop eating that junk food and eat this instead."

"*Maa*, this concoction that you make for me everyday tastes good, but let me tell you something - it's not going to make me look like a white European girl," she asserted.

"That may be true, but this concoction is better for your health than the junk food," Maya responded.

"So… who is coming?" asked Natasha.

"Mr Mathur's family wants to meet you," said Maya.

Natasha knew who Mathurs were. She taunted, "Mathurs, the ones who are shopping for a bride for their son?"

Maya shook her head, "Yes, they are the one."

"*Maa*, you're wasting your time and energy. It's not going to work. Nobody wants a dark skinned bride," gibed Natasha, "Their respect in the community will be diminished if they brought in a dark skinned bride."

Maya interrupted her, "So what if you are dark skinned. You are the most beautiful and talented girl anybody can find."

"So you're going to make me go through that routine once again. Put on layers of makeup to hide my skin, smile and be charming," she scoffed.

"Don't complain. I did this routine many many times when I was at your age."

Natasha shook her head in frustration. "When are they coming?" she asked.

"Tomorrow for dinner," answered Maya, "By the way, I've also called Rucksana from the Beauty Salon. She'll come tomorrow at 5:00 pm to do your makeup."

Natasha rolled her eyes, "I know the drill *Maa*."

CHAPTER XIX

Busted

It was the day of the Mathur's visit. Maya wanted to please them any way she could. She was in the kitchen preparing an elaborate dinner and snacks.

Om entered his house, "Guys, I'm home."

Maya shouted from kitchen, "Om, I need some help. Can you please vacuum the guest room and make sure everything is in place?"

While Om was vacuuming, the doorbell rang. Om looked at his watch and murmured to himself, "They are here already?"

Meanwhile Maya yelled from the kitchen, "Om, can you get the door please?"

Om rushed to do last minute arrangement and examined the room to make sure everything looked right. He opened the door. Rucksana was at the door.

"*Namastey*, I am here to see Mrs. Srivastava," said Rucksana.

"Please come inside," he said. He called for Maya.

Maya looked at the clock in the kitchen. It was 5:00 pm, "Oh, it must be Rucksana," she mumbled. She came out and greeted Rucksana, "Hi Rucksana, please sit down. Natasha is taking a shower and she'll be ready in a minute. Let's go to her room."

Rucksana followed Maya to Natasha's room. Rucksana waited in Natasha's room. Natasha walked out of the bathroom and greeted Rucksana, "Hi Rucksana"

"Hey Natasha"

"So you're here to make me look attractive," taunted Natasha.

Rucksana smiled, "You are already very attractive. I am going to make you look irresistible."

"OK, I'm all yours. Do whatever *Maa* wants," she said.

Rucksana made Natasha sit on a chair in front of a mirror and started to work on her.

"OK, I am going to leave you two girls here and go to kitchen to finish the dinner," said Maya.

After some time the door bell rang again. This time it was Mathur's family.

Om answerd the door bell and greeted Mathurs, "Please come in"

Mr. Mathur, Mrs. Mathur, their son, Ashok, sat on sofa. Meanwhile Maya walked in and greeted everybody. They all sat down.

"Mr. Mathur, you did not bring your daughter?" asked Om.

"My daughter and her hasband were supposed to come this afternoon, but they got stuck in traffic and missed their flight. They are now trying to take an early morning flight."

"Oh, that is too bad," said Om.

"And how is your son? When is he coming to India?" asked Mr. Mathur.

"Vikram is quite busy these days. He will probably come here in a couple of months," Maya answered, "Let me call Natasha."

Maya called for Natasha.

Natasha walked in. Natasha was casually dressed in a *salwar kurta* but she had a very heavy make up which made her skin color look much lighter. She greeted the guests and sat on a separate sofa near Mrs. Mathur. Maya examined Natasha's heavy make up and liked what Rucksana had done. But at the same time she was a little nervous about her makeup. Om felt a little uncomfortable about how Natasha looked. To him, she did not look natural.

Mr. and Mrs. Mathur were surprised to see how Natasha looked. From the pictures that were sent to them, she looked very different. They wondered if she was feeling ok.

"*Betey* Natasha, are you feeling ok?" asked Mr. Mathur.

She quietly nodded her head, "Yes, I am ok."

"You look a little different than your picture," said Mrs. Mathur.

Om knew that he sent the undoctored pictures of Natasha to Mathurs. The heavy makeup made her look very different. Om was a little upset about Natasha's make up but he tried to hide his anger by putting on a smiling face.

Mr. Mathur struck a conversation with Natasha, "How is your work going?"

"There is a lot of work these days. But I am surviving," she answered.

"What are your future plans? Do you want to continue working in your current company?" he asked again.

"I want to work in my current job for at least one more year, and after that I want to do a Ph.D. in computer science and then perhaps look for some teaching and research position in a university," she said.

"That is very nice. Are you also planning to settle abroad?" he asked.

"At this point, I am pretty certain that I will work in India. But I want to get my Ph.D. from the US," she said.

"Why the US?" he asked.

"Well I am already in touch with one professor at MIT, and he has been encouraging me to apply there," she explained, "Let's see how it goes."

"That is an excellent plan," he said admiringly.

Meanwhile, the prospective groom, Ashok, sat there quietly admiring Natasha's beauty and modesty. Mr. Mathur looked at his son and wondered if he needed to ask Natasha anything, "Ashok, why don't you ask Natasha something?"

"In front of everybody?" quipped Ashok.

They all smiled.

"Why don't you guys take a walk in the garden outside while we adults talk here?" Om asked Natasha and Ashok.

Ashok looked at Natasha, "Sure, if it's ok with her."

Natasha and Ashok walked together outside. They were quietly strolling in the garden. It was a small garden with different types of roses. Natasha was uncomfortable about her heavy make up. She did not want Ashok to believe that she was lighter skinned. She decided that she must tell him the truth. Ashok admiringly looked at flowers, smelled them and enjoyed their fragrance.

Ashok broke the ice, "These are beautiful roses. Are they real?"

"The roses are real, but everything that you see in me is not real," she said.

Ashok looked at her curiously wondering what she meant, "Everything in you is not real? What do you mean?"

She knew that any alliance based on deception was doomed to fail. She decided to come clean with him. "Listen, this is the first time we are meeting and I don't know if we will ever meet again," she blurted it out, "Nobody likes to be deceived; therefore, before we proceed any further, you must know that I am a dark skinned girl."

From her pictures that were sent to his family, he already knew that she was dark skinned. He liked her honesty. He decided to have some fun with her, so he pretended to be in shock. "But you don't look like a dark skinned girl," he asked.

"That is what I meant when I said that everything about me is not real. What you see on me is a very heavy make up. I am as dark skinned as my mother," she revealed.

Ashok put on a concerned look on his face and asked, "Are there any more surprises about you?"

"Yes, I've been rejected two times already. Feel free to make any decision, I take rejections quite well," she blurted it out again.

She was now relaxed that she spoke the truth. Ashok, on the other hand was quickly developing a real liking for her beauty and straightforwardness.

He pushed on, "I've heard that you are very smart. Is that real?"

"It's not for me to judge," she responded tersely.

There was a total silence for a few moments. She suspected that like many others, Ashok also had issues with dark skin, and he may feel uncomfortable walking with her after knowing the truth.

She broke the silence. "Let's go inside," she suggested.

"Not so soon, Ms. Unreal," he interrupted her, "You have told your side, you must hear my story too."

He continued, "Let me tell you some things about me too. First, I like your honesty and straightworwardness. The second thing is that I am really color blind. Thirdly, what impresses me most about any person is the person's intelligence and humility. And based on what you have achieved in your career in a short time, you must be very very smart, definitely smarter than me, which is perfectly fine with me."

She looked at him while he continued, "And one more thing, unlike you I don't take rejections well. That means, if I propose to marry you, and if you reject me, I'll quit my job and put up a tent in front of your house and your office and I'll go on hunger strike until you relent. That pretty much sums me up."

Natasha looked at him affectionately and just smiled.

"Are you going to ask me something?" he asked.

Natasha was speechless. After a little pause, she asked, "How close are you to your parents?"

"Very close," he answered.

"Let's say if you choose a girl and your parents do not approve, then what you will do?" she asked.

"If my parents do not approve, I'll not marry," responded Ashok, "But if you were paying any attention to what I said earlier that if I like somebody and my parents do not agree, then I'll go on a hunger strike until my parents relent. You know I've my ways of getting what I want." He smiled and then froze, "Oh, why I'm telling you all these secrets about me. If we get married, you'll know all my tricks."

Natasha smiled shyly but stayed quite.

"Come on, say something," he insisted.

She said, "One way to judge one's character is to see how respectful and caring they are to their parents. Because, if you cannot love your parents, you cannot love anybody, and then you are not worthy of anybody's love."

"Very well said," he said.

"I think we should go inside," she suggested.

"Only on one condition," he said.

"What is it?" she asked.

"We will not make any decisions right now. Let's give each other some more time to determine if we are right for each other. Also, let's try to talk some more," he suggested.

"That is fine. We can talk some more, but I would rather not tell my mother because if she knew that we were chatting then it's very possible that she might get ahead of us and start believing that this was a done deal. And then if things do not work out between us, she'll be hurt again. That means you should also not tell your parents about it either," she suggested.

"But then my parents would want to know my opinion about you," he asked.

Natasha smiled, "I'm sure you're smart enough to deal with the situation."

He smiled.

"OK, let's go inside," she reminded him again.

Ashok and Natasha walked inside. As they walked in, their parents looked at them and smiled.

Maya suspected that something was wrong because she feared that they returned rather quickly, "You guys came back so soon," she wondered.

Ashok stayed quiet. Natasha also did not respond. Maya was worried now.

Meanwhile, Mrs. Mathur turned toward their son, "Ashok and Natasha, do you want to ask each other anything?"

Natasha stayed quiet.

"No, that is OK," said Ashok.

"Then we will take our leave," said Mrs. Mathur.

Mrs. Mathur was little upset about the very heavy make up on Natasha. What she saw in pictures was a natural looking Natasha. But in reality, Natasha appeared fake to her. She was not too sure if Natasha was the right girl for her son. She decided that before she left, she must give them some indication about her displeasure.

"Before we leave, I want to tell Natasha something," said Mrs. Mathur, "Assuming everything in your resume that you sent us is true, you have many accolades to your credit. You have done a remarkable job at a very young age."

Natasha was little annoyed with the statement 'if everything in your resume that you sent us is true'. She twitched with annoyance but decided not to respond to it. Ashok was also a little uncomfortable with that statement. To ease the situation a little, Ashok interrupted, "*Maa*, perhaps she is a modest girl. She probably has more achievements than what is there in her resume."

Mrs. Mathur taunted, "Let's hope so."

There was an uncomfortable silence for a few seconds. Nobody uttered a word. Om could see that Natasha did not like the way Mrs. Mathur spoke about her achievements. He put his arm around Natasha.

"We are going to leave now," Mrs. Mathur declared again.

Maya was worried that these people were leaving without eating dinner. She spent so much time and energy in cooking an elaborate dinner. She suspected the worst.

"Please go after the dinner. You have not eaten anything," she pleaded.

Mrs. Mathur cut her off abruptly, "No thanks, we already ate dinner. Thank you for your hospitality."

Mr. Mathur and Ashok remained quiet but as they left Natasha could clearly see that her mother was disappointed with the way Mrs. Mathur behaved.

As soon as they left, Om was ready to burst. He could not control his anger about Natasha's makeup. Maya was upset too about Mrs. Mathur's rude behavior.

"Mrs. Mathur was so rude," said Maya angrily.

"You know why? Om exploded, "You deceived them about Natasha's skin color."

Maya was shocked to hear Om scream. Om's behavior further fueled Maya's anger, "I did not deceive anybody," she screamed back, "It was just a simple make up. It's perfectly alright for girls to wear makeup. And besides I tried to make her look like the picture that I sent."

Natasha did not want to be part of this. She left the room and went to bathroom where she could hear Om and Maya arguing. She washed off her make up.

Om continued his tirades, "Well first of all, it was not a simple makeup. And secondly, I sent them the correct pictures, not the ones you doctored."

She could not believe what she just heard him say. "You did whaaat…?" she exploded, "You did not send the pictures I gave you?"

Seeing her scream at the top of her voice, he calmed down a little. He lowered his voice a little. "NO," he replied.

Her voice got even louder, "Then which pictures did you send?"

"I sent them the ones you had thrown in the trash," he said.

Now she was completely hysterical, "Oh my God….. Why didn't you tell me that….?" she screamed at the top of her lungs, "If you had told me that I would have done her makeup differently."

He didn't want to lose this battle. He tried to get an upper hand, "So now you admit that your intentions were to hide Natasha's skin. Your intentions were to deceive, wasn't it?"

She started to sob uncontrollably while still screaming, "You deceived me. And if it makes you happy, then, yes I deceived them. I deceived them because I want the best for my child."

He shook his head in outrage, "When you become angry, you become completely irrational, illogical. Do you even realize what you are saying?"

She was still hysterical, "Yes, I know what I am saying. What I am saying is that your actions caused me so much embarrassment. You became a hero but you made me a villain."

Meanwhile Natasha could not tolerate her parents fighting because of her. She barged in the room and intervened, "OK, stop both of you! Whatever happened has happened. You both are overreacting!"

Om started to walk away from the room screaming, "I don't want to be part of these gatherings ever again if we are not going to be honest about everything."

"*Pappa*, please stop," screamed Natasha.

Maya was still crying. She started to walk away to her bedroom while mumbling, "I feel so embarrassed now."

Seeing that Maya had already left the room, Om stayed in the family room and sat on a sofa. He was visibly angry, but perhaps not as hysterical as Maya.

"I'm going to make cold coffee for you guys," said Natasha, "Please drink coffee, cool down and then talk to each other but not about this topic."

After a few minutes, Natasha returned with three glasses of cold coffee. He looked at her, "Give it to your *Maa*. She needs to cool down."

"I'll give one to her too, you take it first," she said.

He took one glass, "Thank you *betey.*"

"You're most welcome, *Pappa*" she said smilingly.

Then she went to her mother's room. Maya was still upset.

"*Maa*, please take this coffee," she said.

Maya looked at Natasha and took coffee. Natasha sat next to Maya, "*Maa*, will you do a favor for me?"

"I know, you are going to ask me to say sorry to your *Pappa*," said Maya grudgingly.

"No, I'm going to bring *Pappa* here and ask him to say sorry to you for not telling you about swapping the pictures. When he says sorry, I want you to say sorry to him for over reacting."

"Did I over react?" asked Maya.

"*Maa*, let's not get into who did what," she appealed, "We need to resolve this otherwise I'll blame myself for being the cause of your fight."

"No *betey*, you are not the cause. It's your father. I feel so embarrassed. What must Mrs. Mathur be thinking about me? He will come out of this a clean man and I'll be the witch," she complained.

"*Maa*, please stop it. Now who is overreacting?" asked Natasha.

Maya quieted down. Natasha put her arm around Maya and tried to calm her down. Natasha lifted Maya's chin and asked, "*Maa*, you'll not dwell on it anymore, will you?"

Maya shook her head.

"So shall I go and work on *Pappa*?" asked Natasha.

Maya again shook her head in affirmation.

Natasha went down where Om was sitting quietly, still upset.

She sat next to him and started to work on him.

"*Pappa*, *Maa* is feeling sorry for how she behaved. Will you now also calm down?" she asked.

Om looked at her for support, "But betey, her arguments for what she did are totally baseless."

"*Pappa*, let's not analyze who said what. I think both of you were overreacting," she told him.

"Was I overreacting?" he asked.

Natasha continued to work on him, "*Pappa*, let's forget that. I've just calmed *Maa* down, please help me resolve the situation, otherwise I'll feel guilty to have caused this argument."

This reasoning of Natasha does the trick. "No betey, you did not cause this. My only mistake was that I did not tell her that I switched the pictures before mailing," he admitted.

She continued to goad him to make up, "Ok *Pappa*, you know that *Maa* is feeling bad. I think you should help her feel better."

"OK I'll apologize to her for not telling her about switching the pictures," he agreed reluctantly.

"So, will you please go to her and handle the situation like the way you always tell us to do?" she asked.

He smiled and gave her a big hug, "*Betey*, what am I going to do when you are gone."

"*Pappa*, I'm not going anywhere," she said.

"And *Pappa*, don't forget to say sorry. Remember you always tell us that 'Love is never hesitating to say sorry'," she rallied him on.

Natasha's prep talk made him feel like he could win anybody. Like a seasoned army general, he stood up and marched toward Maya's room – "OK, here I go, *Inquelab Zindabad*, *Inquelab Zindabad*."

Natasha watched him in praise, gave him thumps up, and smiled. When he reached halfway up the stairs, he turned around, looked at Natasha and said, "If I succeed to conquer her, then we are going out to eat."

"Good. I'll go and get dressed meanwhile," she responded.

Om went in the bedroom upstairs where Maya was sitting quietly. After a couple minutes of apologizing, they both emerged from the bedroom, smiling.

Om called out for Natasha in a loud voice, "*Betey* Natasha, mission accomplished. We are going out to eat."

Natasha emerged smiling from her room dressed up ready to go out. She teased, "I was getting a little worried."

"Why, you lost faith in your father?" he asked.

"It took you almost 90 seconds to accomplish this mission," she teased, "I was about to lose faith in you."

CHAPTER XX

An Arranged Romance

Natasha was in her office when her cellphone rang. She looked at the number of the incoming call. She did not recognize the number. She suspected it to be a prank call and chose not to answer. After a few minutes, the phone rang again. It was the call from the same number. She wondered who it might be. She answered, "Hello."

"Hi, this is Ashok."

"Oh, Hi. I wasn't expecting you to call so soon," she answered blushingly.

"As you can see, patience is not one of my traits. If it's not a good time to call, please let me know I can call at a more convienent time," he said.

"No that's ok, I can talk," she said.

They talked for a long time, and it was clear to both of them that there was something special developing between them.

Natasha looked at her watch. They had been on phone for more than 45 minutes. As much as she wanted to continue talking to him, she knew that she had a lot of thing to do at work.

"We must stop talking before I get fired," she said.

"I didn't realize we have been on phone for 45 minutes," he said, "Time flies when you're having fun."

"I guess so," she concurred, "It was nice talking to you and getting to know you a little better."

Excited about her conversation with Ashok, Natasha quickly called up Vikram.

"Hi sis, what's up?"

"Bhaiyya, I need your help and advice," she said.

"What is it?"

She explained, "There is this guy that *Maa* and *Pappa* like for me. He wants to chat with me on email. I don't know what to write him. Will you help me script my emails?"

"You called the right person. I'm the love guru. I know how guys think," he bragged, "But, first tell me – do you like him?"

"So far, he has passed my preliminary tests," she revealed.

"To have passed your tests, he must be a keeper," he joked.

"Did you already send him an email?" he asked.

"No. I just received an email from him," she said.

Like an expert in relationships, he lectured her, "That is good that you did not make the first move. Guys are like tigers. They like the chase. So play hard to get. Forward that email to me. I'll tell you exactly what to write."

"But keep it to yourself," she told him.

"You got it."

CHAPTER XXI

Flawless Execution

It was four days before the big surprise party. Vikram was supposed to be arriving in India with Megan the next day. Natasha was in her office making final arrangements for the party. She heard a beeping on her computer. It was Vikram trying to set up a video chat with her. She answered, "Hi brother"

"Sis, here is the plan. Megan and I are arriving there tomorrow night. I'll take a taxi and go to *Dadi Maa*'s house directly. My plan is to stay at *Dadi Maa*'s for two days and then directly show up for the big party."

Natasha was anxious to meet her brother and Megan.

"No, you'll not take the taxi. I'll bring our car to the airport," she said, "Besides; I'm dieing to see Megan."

The plan had been working flawlessly so far. He did not want to take any chances.

"But then *Maa* and *Pappa* will wonder where you're going in the night," he wondered.

By now, Natasha had become an expert in deception. She assured him, "Don't worry, compared to what we have been able to pull off so far, this will be a walk in the park. I'll make some excuse."

"OK, whatever you do, but please don't spoil the surprise," he warned.

"Don't worry. By the way, does *Dadi Maa* know about Megan?" she asked.

"Oh yes, I've told her everything. She is excited to meet her. I've already sent her Megan's picture," he said excitedly.

"How is the preparation going?" he wondered.

"Everything is in place. The hall is booked, the menu is almost finalized, and all the friends of *Maa* and *Pappa* have been contacted. You just come here soon," she told him.

"OK, then I'll see ya soon. Bye."

Natasha was incredibly excited and had already cooked up a plan to cover up her trip to airport. As soon as Vikram hung up, she called her friend Shweta.

"Shweta, tomorrow is your birthday," said Natasha.

Shweta was surprised to hear that. She corrected her, "No, tomorrow is not my birthday."

"No, it's your birthday tomorrow," Natasha insisted, "And you're taking some friends out for dinner."

"Natasha, please tell me what is going on," asked Shweta suspecting that Natasha was up to something,

"I've to go pick up *Bhaiyya* at the airport tomorrow. Thus I need an excuse to leave the house so I can go to the airport," she explained.

Shweta laughed, "Natasha, after all this is over, you should write a book on deception. You're getting good at it."

"Of course I'll write a book, but before that you call me at my home tonight exactly at 7:00 pm," she instructed with a laugh, "I'll make sure that either *Maa* or *Pappa* pick up the phone. Whoever is on the phone, tell that person about dinner that you're planning at around 7:00 pm."

"Oh, this is so exciting. But are we really meeting for dinner?" asked Shweta.

"No, there is no dinner. I'll go directly to the airport," she said, "OK, I've to run; someone else is calling me."

* * *

Natasha, Maya and Om were at home watching TV. Vikram was arriving the next day, and Maya and Om were totally clueless about it.

Natasha headed for bathroom as the clock was to strike seven, and as soon as Natasha left, the telephone rang.

"Hello Auntie, this is Shweta," greeted Shweta.

"Oh hi Shweta, how are you?" asked Maya.

"I am good. How are you?" said Shweta.

"We are all doing well," replied Maya.

"I was calling to see if Maya is free tomorrow evening," said Shweta enacting her part.

"What is happening tomorrow?" she asked.

"Oh, not much," she read from a script, "Tomorrow is my birthday. I thought it'll be good excuse to take my close friends out to dinner."

"That is great! Happy Birthday!"

Shweta twitched her eyes because it was actually not her birthday. "Thank you," she said in a low voice.

Natasha had been timing this conversation. She came out of the bathroom at just the right time. Seeing Natasha come out of bathroom, Maya handed the phone to her, "Shweta, here is Natasha."

Natasha took the phone, "Hi Shweta"

"Bla, bla, bla, bla, bla, bla, bla, bla, bla, bla, bla…," blabbered Shweta.

"Oh, tomorrow at 7:00 pm. Sure. Happy birthday," said Natasha ignoring her blabber.

"Bla, bla, bla, bla, bla, bla, bla, bla, bla, bla, bla…," Shweta continued.

Natasha decided to have some fun with Shweta too.

"So how old are you?" she asked.

"Bla, bla, bla, bla, bla, bla, bla, bla, bla, bla, bla…," Shweta continued.

Natasha pretended to be shocked, "Oh really? I must say you're doing an excellent job hiding your age."

Meanwhile Maya looked at Natasha with amusement.

Shweta stopped her blabbering, "You'll pay for this," said Shweta grinding her teeth.

Natasha ignored her and continued with her scripted part, "Let me check my appointment book."

She opened her bag and took out her appointment book and flipped its pages pretending to look at her appointment schedule. "I've nothing going on tomorrow evening," she said.

Shweta resumed her blabbering, "Bla, bla, bla, bla, bla, bla, bla, bla, bla, bla, bla..."

Natasha responded, "But let me ask *Maa* if she has any plans."

Natasha turned toward her *Maa*, "Do we have anything planned for tomorrow evening."

"Betey, it's your friend's birthday. Go and be a part of her celebration," said Maya.

"OK Shweta, I can come tomorrow," said Natasha.

"Bla, bla, bla, bla, bla, bla, bla, bla, bla, bla, bla...," Shweta continued.

Natasha decided to have some more fun with Shweta, "Thank you for inviting me. What do you want for your birthday gift?"

"Your head," said Shweta.

Natasha continued with her gag, "Just my good wishes! Ok, I'll see you tomorrow."

"Bla, bla, bla, bla, bla, bla, bla, bla, bla, bla, bla….."

"Bye."

CHAPTER XXII

Anticipation

Natasha was at the airport waiting for Vikram and Megan, and as soon as Vikram and Megan emerged, Natasha ran towards them. The first thing she noticed was that Megan was as dark as she was. She was a beautiful African American lady, and while Natasha was happy for her brother, she also grimaced at what she knew what a difficult time Vikram would have explaining Megan to Mom.

Natasha hugged Vikram and then turned toward Megan, "Hi Megan."

"Hi Natasha"

"You're much more beautiful than your picture," said Natasha.

Megan blushed, "Oh thank you."

"So, are you guys ready for the acting job of your life?" asked Natasha.

"I'm ready to go," he said excitedly.

"I'm more nervous than ready," said Megan.

Natasha reassured her, "Don't worry about it. It'll be a lot of fun."

"I hope I can pull it off," said Megan.

"Don't worry about it. Just fasten your seat belt and enjoy the ride," he said.

As soon as they came out of the airport, Vikram took a deep breath, "Oh, home sweet home!"

They put their baggage in the car.

"Natasha, give me the car key, let me drive," he said.

"Are you sure?" she asked as he nodded and took the keys from her hands.

"Megan, come on. Let's sit together on the back seat," suggested Natasha.

He looked at them strangely, "So I'm going to be your chauffeur?"

"You'll have to be if you want me to help you in your scheme," said Natasha.

"Yes Ms. Blackmail, I guess I'm your slave while I'm here," he gibed with a laugh as he started the car and weaved through the nightmarish airport traffic while Megan looked outside curiously.

About an hour later the three arrived at their grandmother's house. She was anxiously waiting for Vikram and Megan.

The grand mother opened the door when she heard the sound of their car. She was ecstatic to see Vikram, "Oh, my child Vickie. I've been waiting for so long."

Vikram touched his *Dadi Maa*'s feet[3] and gave her a tight hug. Then *Dadi Maa* turned toward Megan, "And this pretty lass must be Megan.

As instructed, Megan touched *Dadi Maa*'s feet. *Dadi Maa* immediately hugged her and blessed her, "God bless you my child."

"Oh, you are so beautiful," said *Dadi Maa* lovingly while pinching Megan's cheeks.

"*Dadi Maa*, can I also get a hug?" said Natasha, feeling left out.

"Oh my child, come here," said *Dadi Maa*, "How can I forget you?"

"OK, let's go inside," said *Dadi Maa,* "Go and freshen up. I've made some of your favorite food."

Natasha could not stay long because otherwise her parents would start calling Shweta's house. She asked to be excused, "*Dadi Maa*, I'll have to go because *Maa* and *Pappa* think that I'm having dinner with my friend Shweta."

"Oh, it'll be just a few minutes. Everything is ready," she insisted.

"If I don't reach there by 11:00 pm, they will start calling Shweta and then the whole secret will be out," warned Natasha.

"Ok just take some snacks and you can eat them while driving," suggested her grandmother.

"OK guys, get some rest. We have a lot of activities planned for tomorrow," Natasha reminded them, "We are meeting at Tullu *Chacha*'s house for our first live music practice."

"What about Megan?" wondered Vikram.

"Shweta will take Megan out for lunch and sightseeing and also tutor her a little about my work if in case somebody decides to quiz her," she explained, "Remember, she is supposed to be my colleague from work?"

"Yes, of course," said Vikram while everybody chuckled.

3 People show their respect to their elders by touching their feet.

Natasha's cellphone rang. It was her father calling. She signaled everybody to be quiet. She answered the phone, "Yes, Pappa."

"Betey Natasha, When will you be home?" asked Om.

"*Pappa*, I'm driving. I should be there in half an hour," she said.

"OK, drive carefully," advised Om.

She shut her phone, "OK, guys I got to run. See you tomorrow." said Natasha while running outside to her car.

CHAPTER XXIII

Final Preparation

The next day Natasha was in her office, when her computer beeped signaling a new message. It was an email from Ashok. Natasha smiled and read his email. Natasha and Ashok were coming closer through their frequent emails. They had developed quite a fondness for each other. After she responded to Ashok's email, she called *Dadi Maa*'s house, "*Dadi Maa*, how is it going?"

"These guys are still sleeping. We were talking till 2:00 am last night," she said.

"Ha, knowing *bhaiyya* I could have guessed that," she said with a laugh, "Anyway, please get them and yourself ready. Shweta is going to pick all of you guys up and drop you and *Bhaiyya* to Tullu *Chacha*'s house and take Megan out to lunch."

"I'll wake them up right now."

* * *

Natasha had already made arrangements for a final live music session at Atul's home. It was lunch time and Natasha had already reached Tullu's house and they were all waiting on Vikram's arrival.

"Knock, Knock."

Atul ran to open the door and let Vikram and his grandmother in. Everyone was excited to see Vikram and as soon as he entered he greeted his uncle and aunt and took their blessings.

While all this was happening, Radha was quietly standing in another corner of the room waiting to get Vikram's attention. After greeting everyone else, Vikram looked around for Radha. He spotted her standing in a corner. Without saying anything he opened his arms and slowly started to walk toward her. She continued to stand there for a few moments and then charged toward him and gave him a big hug. She was ecstatic seeing him after several years.

"Oh, Vickie, you look the same," she said joyfully.

He examined her from head to toe, "And where is the rest of you?"

She looked him curiously not knowing what he meant. "What do you mean?" she asked.

"What I recall there was more of you two years ago when I saw you last. Now you look like you are on a hunger strike," he clarified.

"I just wanted to lose some weight before you came," she revealed.

Natasha interrupted them, "Guys, we can talk later. But let's do what we came here for. I've to go back to work."

"Yes, let's get to work," said Atul.

CHAPTER XXIV

No Celebration?

It was a day before the big anniversary party. Om, Maya and Natasha were relaxing in their living room. Natasha decided to break the silence and struck a conversation with them about their upcoming 25th marriage anniversary.

"*Maa*, I'm planning a liitle party on your anniversary tomorrow," she said.

Maya did not want have any party due to obvious reasons – first, she knew that her son was not going to be there, and secondly, he didn't even remember her anniversary.

"No, I told you there will not be any celebration unless my entire family is here," she asserted.

Om was not that stubborn. "But we have to do something," he said.

Realising that it was very important day in their life, Maya relented for doing something.

"OK, we'll go out to eat," she declared.

Natasha pushed on, "But what about the party?"

"No party," she proclaimed.

Then Natasha's cellphone rang. She did not recognize the number. She answered the phone, "Hello."

"Maam, I am calling from the Zaika Catering sevice," said a man on the other end.

Natasha looked around to make sure nobody was listening. Maya and Om were away in the the other corner of the room. She concluded that if she talked softly they will not be able to hear her.

"Yes?" she asked.

"I wanted to know what type of ice cream you want to be served tomorrow. We have vanilla, chocolate, mango and peach flavors," said the man.

Natasha tried to find words without letting Maya and Om know about it. "Let's do the first two, half and half," she instructed.

Both Om and Maya could hear Natasha. They wondered what she could be discussing.

"You mean vanilla and chocolate?" asked the man.

"Yes."

The man had one more question, "And what kind of toppings do you want on the icecream? We have coconut, cookies, cashews, pistachios."

"Let's do the last two, half and half," she instructed.

"You mean cashews and pistachios both?" he asked.

"Yes"

"Thank you Maam," he hung up wondering why she responded this way.

Once Natasha hung up, Maya inquired, "Who was it?"

Natasha quickly thought of another cover up, "Oh it was one of my friends. She was asking about the recipe to make *Gulab Jamun*. I told her to use Milk Powder and suger, half and half."

"No, that is not right. You don't mix milk powder and sugar half and half," said Maya, "Please call her and tell her the correct recipe."

Natasha tried to ward her off, "I'll tell her tomorrow. She is going to make them tomorrow anyway."

Maya wondered and shook her head, "You have made *gulab jamun* so many times. How could you forget its recipe?" said Maya.

Natasha just shrugged.

Maya then turned toward Om, "I think you should bring *Maa Ji* (Om's mother) to our house tomorrow. We can all go out to eat."

"I think that is great idea. I'll call her right now," he responded delightfully.

Om called his mother. She was in the kitchen making *pakoris*. She was not expecting a call from Om. She asked Vikram to answer the phone. Vikram did not realize that it was his father at the other end. He answered the phone, "Hello"

"Hello," said Om.

Hearing a male voice, Om suspected that perhaps he dialed a wrong number. Vikram recognized that it was his *Pappa*. He quickly put his hand on the speaker and whispered to Megan, "It's *Pappa*."

Om checked to make sure he dialed the right number, "Is it 729356?"

Vikram put a piece of cloth on the speaker and tried to alter his voice. He pretended to be a house cleaner who did not know English very well. He responded in broken English, "Yes, doo you baant tu tawk tu *Maa Ji*?"

Megan was standing right next to Vikram. She was thoroughly amused seeing this. She tried to control her laughter.

"Yes, but who are you?" asked Om.

"Sir, my name eez Chhedi Lal. I am houz kleener. *Maa jee* caalled me tu kleen houz," he responded in broken English.

Om was a little baffled. He whispered to himself, "Clean the house in the night?"

Meanwhile Vikram ran to *Dadi Maa* to tell her about the phone call.

"*Dadi Maa*, it is *Pappa*," he whispered, "I told him that my name is Chhedi Lal and I am a house cleaner."

Dadi Maa and Megan laughed.

Dadi Maa washed her hands and answered the phone pretending she did not know who it was, "Hello?"

"*Maa*, how are you?" asked Om.

"Oh Om, I am good," said *Dadi Maa* acting surprised to hear from him.

"Who was that man?" he asked.

Controlling her laugh, she answered, "Oh Chhedi Lal? The house needed some cleaning so I called him."

"Cleaning in the night?" he probed.

She was ready with a convincing answer, "You know *beta*, it's difficult to get good house cleaners these days. He is generally very busy during day time. He only has time during the nights."

"But why was he talking in English?" Om probed again.

"Oh, I am teaching him to speak English," she answered.

Om was baffled but appeared to be satisfied with this answer.

"Well *Maa*, Maya and I want you to spend tomorrow with us," he told her.

"Oh yes, tomorrow is your 25th marriage anniversary," she said.

"Yes. Shall I pick you up at 10:00 in the morning?" he asked.

She purposely tried to suggest him otherwise, "I think you should have a quiet time with Maya and Natasha tomorrow."

Om ignored her advice, "*Maa* I'll come tomorrow to pick you up at 10:00."

"I know you'll not take no for an answer, so I'll be ready," she said.

"Did you talk to Vikram lately?" she asked trying to keep herself from laughing.

"Yes, we talked to him about 3 days ago, said Om, "He said he will be travelling for the entire week so he may not be able to call us regularly. But I am sure he will call tomorrow."

"It would have been so nice if he had come here too," she said while adding sadness to her voice.

"I know, but I guess work is more important than our anniversary," he said.

"OK, when he calls tomorrow, please let me talk to him too," she suggested.

"OK," he said, "So I'll see you tomorrow."

As *Dadi Maa* put down the phone, Vikram looked around and proceeded to walk out the window and looked down the road to where the party would be.

"Yes *Pappa*, I guess you will."

CHAPTER XXV

More Tricks

It was the day of Om and Maya's anniversary. Natasha woke up and went to her parent's bedroom.

"Happy Anniversary!" she said as she entered their room.

"Oh thank you *betey,*" they said as they got out of bed and hugged Natasha. Maya and Om were not very excited about their anniversary because they knew that on this important day their son would not be with them.

"I am going to pick up *Maa*," Om said

"You told her 10 O'Clock, and it's only 8 O'Clock," Maya told him.

"I am already ready, and I might as well go otherwise I well get stuck in traffic," he explained.

"OK, please pick up some *samosas* from Ramlal's shop on your way back. *Maa ji* likes them," she told him.

Om was excited about samosa, "Yum, I like them too."

He arrived at his mother's house at 9:00 am. He rang the doorbell.

Vikram, Megan and *Dadi Maa* were sitting at breakfast table sipping morning tea. *Dadi Maa* looked at the clock. It was only 9 O'Clock. She was not sure who it might be. She signaled Vikram and Megan by putting her finger on her mouth, "Everbody quiet! It may be Om."

She quietly tiptoed to near her window and peeped outside to see who it was. Seeing Om standing outside she got panicky, "Oh my god, it is Om. Come on, everybody hide."

Vikram and Megan scrambled for a place to hide. They quickly went under the breakfast table and hid behind the long table cover. Meanwhile, *Dadi Maa* tried to clear the breakfast table.

Om rang the doorbell again.

"I am coming," she called out.

She opened the door. Om touched her feet and she blessed him while at the same time side glancing to where Vikram and Megan were hiding to make sure they were well hidden. She was a very nervous. "*Maa*, are you feeling OK?" asked Om.

"I am fine, why?" she snapped.

"You just seem a little anxious about something," he told her.

She tried the compose herself, "Anxious? Oh No No. I am fine, I am fine."

Om shrugged his shoulders, "OKaaayyy"

"I am ready. Let me just pick up my bag," she told him.

"Can I drink a cup of tea?" he asked.

She was afraid that if he stayed he would find out who was hiding behind the table cover. She was anxious to leave the house, "No, we'll drink tea with Maya."

Om wondered again about his mother's unusual behavior, but put it off as nothing.

She picked up her bag. She wanted to give some instruction to Vikram before leaving her house. She spoke in a loud voice pretending to talk to herself, "Let me see where my house keys are. I always keep one key with me and the other key on the top shelf of the refrigerator."

Om wondered about his mother, "*Maa*, are you telling this to the walls?"

She pretended to be annoyed, "Yes, I am talking to walls. Living alone makes you talk to walls."

Om shook his head while she continued to speak in a loud voice, "Whenever I leave the house I always make sure that all the lights are off, all doors are locked."

"That is good *Maa*," he said, "Let's go now."

She continued to speak in a loud voice, "There is a lot of food in the refrigerator that two people can easily eat."

Om was a little miffed, "I am sure *Maa*, but you are eating at our house."

She continued to give instructions to Vikram hiding under that table, "I normally take taxi to go to your house from the intersection. I never pay more than 150 Rs."

Om got a little irritated on why his mother was telling him all this, "*Maa*, we are not going in a taxi. What has happened to you?"

She ignored him and started to walk outside with him. When they were just outside the door, she quickly turned around, "Om, you wait here, let me make sure I locked all the doors."

Om waited near the door.

She quickly went near the table and bent down to give instructions to Vikram and Megan while also side glancing at the door to make sure that Om was not watching, "OK children, I am leaving. Make sure you lock all the doors. The keys are in the top shelf of the refrigerator. There is food in the fridge."

Om walked in while *Dadi Maa* was whispering to Vikram and Megan. As soon as she saw Om, she pretended to be looking for her sandles.

"*Maa*, are you looking for something?" he asked.

"I am looking for my sandles," she snapped back.

"*Maa*, you already have sandles on," said Om.

She looked down at her feet and faked a smile, "Oh yes, you know, memory is the first thing that quits you when you get old."

He again shook his head in bewilderment.

They again started to walk outside. As soon as she was about to get out of the door, she said, "Bye house; bye refrigerator; bye furniture; and bye everybody else."

Om was bewildered again and did not know why his mother was behaving this way. He finally sat in his car. She sat on the passenger seat. As soon as the car started to drive off, Vikram and Megan ran to the window. She looked up to the window and they waved hands to each other and smiled.

"Are you saying bye again to your house?" he asked sarcastically.

"Yes *beta*," she said pretending to act foolish.

Om was worried that his mother might be loosing her mind in her old age.

"*Maa*, I think you should live with us," he suggested.

She knew exactly why he suggested that. She was relieved that he did not suspect anything.

"*Beta*, I want to keep working. That is the only way to keep this body fit. If I go to your house, Maya and you will not let me work and I know when I stop working I will be as good as dead."

CHAPTER XXVI

Surprise! Surprise!

It was the evening of the party. The whole secret was going to be revealed in about an hour. Om and Maya had no clue as to what the evening was going to be like. They were just planning for a quite dinner with their daughter and Om's mother.

Maya was deeply disappointed that Vikram did not even call to wish them happy anniversary. "How he could forget that," she wondered.

Meanwhile, Vikram and all the guests had already arrived at the Gymkhana Club gardens, and were ready for the party.

Natasha came out of her room all dressed up. Her father and grandmother were already ready, but Maya was not there. "*Maa*, please come soon," she called for her *Maa*, "We have a reservation at 6:00 pm."

"I'll be right out," she said.

Maya came out in few seconds. She asked Natasha if Vikram called.

"*Maa* I've already left a message for him. When he gets time, he will call," she said.

"Please try him one more time," Maya insisted.

Natasha pressed some fake numbers and held the phone in her ears.

A recorded message played on the phone, "The number you have dialed is not a valid number. Please check your number and dial again."

She pretended that Vikram was not responding. She spoke into the phone pretending to leave a message for Vikram, "*Bhaiyya*, please call when you get this message. *Maa* and *Pappa* want to talk to you. And please call at my cellphone because we are not going to be home for next several hours. It's about 5:30 right now. Bye, don't work too hard."

Natasha turned to her mother, "Are you satisfied now?"

"Yes," said Maya.

They arrived at the restaurant. They left their car for valet parking and proceeded inside the restaurant. Natasha took the lead and talked to the attendant. She had already talked to the restaurant manager and he knew about her plan. The attendant looked for her name and then asked them to follow him. The attendant sat them at a table. Maya still could not accept that Vikram did not call yet.

"Natasha! Is your cellphone on?" she asked.

"Yes, it's on, *Maa*," said Natasha pretending to be irritated.

"Is it charged?" she asked again.

"Yes *Maa* it's charged," she replied.

At that point, according to the plan, her grandmother got up to go to the bathroom. But instead of going to the bathroom, she joined all the party members already there in the garden of the Club located at the back of the restaurant. Now there were only three of them there.

Natasha looked around. There were people sitting in booths. She pretended that booth seating was better than where they were seated.

"Booth seating is better, isn't it?" she asked her parents.

"Let's just sit here. This is fine," said Maya.

"Wait here. Let me talk to the restaurant manager," said Natasha while leaving them there and pretending to go to see the manager.

Now Om and Maya were there sitting alone in the restaurant. Natasha joined the party crowd in the garden. The garden was decorated with "Happy 25th Anniversary" banners. Vikram and Megan were there too. Natasha went there and announced to everybody, "Guys, everything is going exactly according to the plan. *Maa* and *Pappa* should be here any moment."

Then she turned toward Vikram, "*Bhaiyya*, if you want to highten the climax some more you can hide behind this tree."

Meanwhile, inside the restaurant, according to the plan, a waiter approached Om and Maya.

"Sir, your daughter has chosen a table in the garden. Please follow me," he said.

Om looked around for his mother, "But my mother is in the bathroom."

"No sir, she is already their in the garden," he said, "Ms. Natasha already took her there."

They followed the waiter.

All the lights in the garden were purposely turned off. The garden was totally dark. Using a flash light, the waiter led Om and Maya into the garden.

They wondered why it was so dark there.

Then suddenly backyard was completely lit.

SURPRISE!! SURPRISE!! HAPPY ANNIVERSARY!!

Om and Maya were totally shocked to see so many people there. They did not know how to react. Maya was happy, but she was still thinking why Vikram had not called yet.

The guests wished them on their anniversary. Maya and Om were delighted to see all their friends and family.

"Oh my god who did all this," she asked.

Natasha smiled, "*Maa* you'll find out soon."

Natasha stood next to her mother, and then suddenly her cellphone rang. Hearing the phone ring, Maya perked up. She asked her to check to see if it was Vikram's call.

Natasha checked her phone. It was Vikram calling from behind a tree.

It was time to reveal the big secret. "*Maa*, it is *Bhaiyya*," said Natasha excitedly.

Maya and Om's faces lit up. Natasha switched her phone to the speaker mode.

"I knew that he would call," she said proudly while grabbing the phone from Natasha.

"Betey Vikram, where were you. We left you so many messages," she said.

Vikram wished them "*Maa* and *Pappa*, a very very happy 25th anniversary!"

"Thank you, *beta*, you'll not believe what Natasha has done here. I did not want any party without you," she told him.

"*Maa* and *Pappa*, No matter which part of the world I was, I would have never missed this day," he said.

"Oh *beta*, you have called me, I am so happy now. It must be early in the morning in America," she said.

Vikram decided to play some more with his mother, "No *Maa*, it's about 6:30 in the evening here."

Maya was confused, "How can it be 6:30 pm there, it is 6:30 pm here."

Om was listening to there conversation. He started to get the inkling that something was strange. He could hear Vikram's voice coming from behind the tree. He leaned to get the glimpse of person standing behind the tree. He made an eye contact with Vikram.

Om screamed with joy as loud as he could, "OH MY GOD, VICKIE IS HERE!!!!!"

Maya turned around and saw Vikram smiling behind the tree. She could not contain her joy and excitement. She just stood there frozen not believing her eyes. Vikram ran to her. Her eyes dampened with tremendous joy. She hugged him so tight as if to never let go.

"How did you pull this off?" asked Om.

"With the help of *Dadi Maa*, Sis, Tullu *Chacha* and *Chachi*, and Katori," he said.

"So you were there when I picked up *Maa*," he inquired.

"Yes," said Vikram.

"I knew something smelled fishy but I did not know that you were the fish," said Om.

Natasha chimed in, "*Maa*, it was all his idea. He was the captain of the ship and we were all his workers. We did exactly what he said."

"Looks like everybody knew about this party except us," said Om.

"That is why it's called a surprise party," added Vikram's grand mother.

At a distance, Megan was standing with Shweta watching all this.

It was now time for the next act.

Natasha approached Megan to prep her up for her part. "Do you remember your part or do you need a quick rehearsal?" she whispered into Megan's ears.

"If I do any more rehearsals, I'll get more nervous. So let's try it as is," said Megan nervously.

Both Megan and Natasha walked to her parents.

She introduced Megan to her parents, "*Maa*, this is Megan. She is from the US and she has recently joined our company."

Megan folded her hands and Maya reciprocated.

"Where are you from in the US?" asked Om.

"I live in Philadelphia," she replied.

"Have you met my son Vikram?" he asked, "He also lives in Philadelphia."

"Yes, I've met him," she told him, "You must be proud to have him as your son and Natasha as your daughter."

Natasha excused herself, "OK I'll let you guys talk. I'll go and get ready for few more surprises."

Om looked at her, "Are there more surprises?"

She walked away smiling.

While Om, Maya and Megan continued to talk, Natasha, Vikram, Radha, *Dadi Maa*, Tullu *Chacha* and Chachi huddled to get ready to play their song.

Maya looked at them huddling. She asked Megan, "What are these guys up to now?"

"Looks like they are getting ready for some kind of stage performance," said Megan.

At that time Vikram took the mike and spoke, "Can I've your attention please?"

Everbody turned toward Vikram.

Vikram began his speech, "First of all I want to thank everybody who helped me pull this off. Especially, my *Dadi Maa*, my beautiful sister, my childhood friend, Dr. Radha Kumar, and my *chacha* and *chachi*."

He continued, "And thank you Shweta for all you have done."

He resumed, "OK now *Maa* and *Pappa*, congratulation on your 25th anniversary."

Everybody joined in the applause.

He continued addressing his parents, "*Maa* and *Pappa*, I apologize for playing with your emotions throughout the last few weeks. I knew everytime I told you that I was not coming, I was causing you pain. But when we saw the joy on your faces this evening, it was all worth it. *Pappa* you have always told us that 'Love is never hesitating to say you're sorry' so on behalf all those who were part of this scheme I say – *Maa* and *Pappa* we're sorry to have caused you anguish during the last two weeks. You guys have done so much not only for Sis, Katori and I, but you have also changed many others lives as well."

Everybody clapped again. Maya's eyes dampened with emotions. Om delivered a flying kiss to Vikram.

Vikram continued, "I think Natasha will agree with me that we are fortunate to have parents like you."

Dadi Maa yelled from the audience, "Can I take some credit for giving your father the excellent training?"

Vikram smiled, "*Dadi Maa*, of course! You're our role model. We are what we are because of you."

Om, Tullu *Chacha*, Natasha, and Maya led the clapping. Everybody joined in.

Vikram continued, "With that I would like to present to you something. With the help of Sis, Katori – by the way if some of you don't know who Katori is, she is Dr. Radha Kumar; and also please note, that only I'm allowed to address her with this name."

Natasha interjected and yelled, "I can call her Katori too."

Then *Dadi Maa* shouted, "Me too"

Om followed suit, "And me too"

Radha smiled, and while the commotion continued she went up to the stage and took the mike from Vikram.

"OK, if you call me Katori, then you'll have to love me as much as Vickie does. Please raise your hands if you agree to this," announced Radha.

Everybody raised their hands. She was thrilled to see so many raised hands.

"Ok, so from now onwards I'm no longer Dr. Radha Kumar. I'm Katori to not only Vikram, but to you all too," she proclaimed.

After that there was a prolonged applause led by Vikram.

She handed over the mike back to Vikram and joined the crowd of guests.

Vikram resumed his speech, "Ok now that we have resolved this, let me get back to what I was saying earlier. So again – *Maa* and *Pappa*, with the help of Natasha, Dr. Katori, *Dadi Maa*, Tullu *Chacha* and *Chachi*, we have composed this song just for you. And also please note that none of us do music for living so don't expect us to do wonders."

Everybody applauded. Maya and Om's eyes were damp with happy emotions. They were speechless.

Vikram invited all the musicians and singers on the stage? Natasha strapped on the base guitar, Radha stood behind the keyboard, *Dadi Maa* sat down with the *dholak*, and Tullu *Chacha* sat with the tabla. Vikram, holding the lead guitar looked around at all the musician.

"Is everybody ready?" he asked. All the musicians gave thumbs up.

Vikram looked at his parents, "OK *Maa* and and *Pappa*, this one is for you. 1, 2, 3…"

* * *

After the song, the party slowly wound down and the guests slowly left. The ones who were still there were *Dadi Maa*, Katori and her husband, Shweta, Megan, Natasha, Vikram, and Maya and Om.

Vikram winked at Natasha and *Dadi Maa* to play out the next act.

Natasha approached Megan and spoke to her in loud enough voice so Maya and Om could hear her, "Megan, where are you going tonight?"

Megan called up from her script, "To my hotel."

Natasha pretended to be surprised, "To your hotel? But it's so late in the night!"

Natasha's loud voice attracted Maya's and Om's attention. She immediately approached Megan, "No you're not going to any hotel. You're coming with us to our house. This is the first time you have come to our country. You must experience living with an Indian family."

Vikram clinched his fists in triumph of how well the plan was working. Natasha, *Dadi Maa*, and Vikram looked at each other and secretly acknowledged the flawless excecution of the plan.

Like a good student, Megan recited the next line from her script, "Thank you very much for the offer, and I would love to come to your house, but you have not seen Vickie in two years, and I think you should spend time with your family."

"Our family is very big," Om chimed in, "All of Natasha's friends and all of Vickie's friends are our family."

"Megan, you'll make us very happy if you spend a few days with us," said Maya.

To give more credibility to their plan, Vikram and Natasha also appealed to Megan for her to stay with them.

Natasha decided to have some fun and blurted out a line that was not part of the script, "We promise not to bombard you with Indian food and spices."

Without thinking, Megan quickly responded, "No I'm not afraid of Indian spices. In fact I've learnt to cook with Indian spices. And I think I'm not that bad, wouldn't you say Vickie?"

Vikram twitched his eyes fearing that Megan's statement might have exposed their relationship. Megan also immediately realized that she spoke too much. Maya and Om wondered what she meant, but before Maya and Om could suspect anything Vikram tried to change the subject.

"Yes, Sis told me that you're an excellent cook," said Vikram, "OK, so it's decided. Megan is coming with us."

"But I still have to go to hotel to get my clothes," said Megan.

Natasha jumped in, "Oh you can wear my clothes; we are almost the same size. I think my clothes will fit you perfectly."

Om again chimed in, "When in India, wear as Indians do, and eat as Indians do."

"OK, I guess I'll stay with you all tonight," said Megan.

Vikram then pleaded his *Dadi Maa* to stay with him for some more time.

"*Betey*, I already got to spend time with you alone. Now let you parents enjoy you," she said.

"Just a couple of days, please," he pleaded again.

"You guys have power to make me do anything," she said as they all left for home.

CHAPTER XXVII

The Cat Is Out Of The Bag

It was about 8 am in the morning. Everybody, except Vikram was up. Maya and Natasha were preparing snacks in the kitchen while Megan was watching them attentively. Maya washed vegetables in the sink while Natasha made *halwa*. Natasha wore a *salwar-kurta*. Megan also wore one of Natasha's *salwar-kurta*. It fitted her perfectly.

After Natasha finished frying the flour, she put water in the frying pan. Megan wondered – "Don't you put milk after you finish frying?"

"Yes, you can make it both ways. I was trying to make it light in calories," she explained.

"Megan, do you know how to make *halwa*?" Maya asked Megan.

"Yes, I've tried it a few times," she answered.

While Maya was not looking at them, Megan whispered into Natasha's ears, "I've made it a few times for Vickie."

Both of them giggled quietly.

"What are you two girls giggling about?" asked Maya.

"It is girl-talk *Maa*," responded Natasha while giggling some more.

"OK, after you finish giggling please go and wake up Vickie otherwise he will sleep till noon," said Maya.

Natasha handed over the spatula to Megan for her to continue stirring while she went to Vikram's room to wake him up.

Meanwhile, Maya called for Om to come to the kitchen.

Om walked in the kitchen wearing a white *kurta-paijama*.

"Om, can you please go and get *samosas* and *jalebi*?" she asked.

He turned toward Megan, "Megan, please stay with us for a few days because as long as you are here, I'll get to get to eat what I love."

Megan laughed. Maya smiled and shook her head at Om's sense of humor.

"With this kind of attention and hospitality, I'll be crazy to leave anytime soon," she acknowledged.

At that instant Vikram walked into the kitchen wearing a white *kurta-paijama*. He sniffed around, "I smell *halwa*."

Maya looked at Vikram suscipiciously, "Vickie, you came down so quickly. Did you brush your teeth?"

Vikram pretended to be aggravated, "*Maaaa*, I'm not 6 year old little boy any more. Yes, I did brush my teeth and that too for full 5 minutes. I brushed my tongue too, see." He pulled his tongue out and turned toward his mother. Then he turned toward Megan and again pulled his tongue out. "Do you want to see it too Megan?" he asked.

"No thanks. I'll pass," said Megan while turning her head away.

Vikram then joked with Megan, "Megan, aren't you glad that she is not your mom?"

"What happened?" interjected Maya, "Yesterday in the party you were saying that you have the best parents."

Om interrupted, "OK guys, you continue arguing; I'll go and get *samosas* and *jalebi*."

Hearing that they were going to have *samosas* and *jalebis* Vikram perked up, "*Pappa*, I'll come with you."

"Megan, why don't you also go with them," suggested Maya, "You can see the market. Natasha and I'll manage here, unless Natasha wants to go too."

"No, I'll get breakfast ready," said Natasha.

Om, Vikram, and Megan left.

To get a better view of the town while driving, Om asked Megan to sit in front. Vikram drove the car while Om sat on the back seat. As Vikram impressed Megan with his driving skills, she looked outside intently. The whole town was bustling with activities - dogs were running freely; everybody was moving and going somewhere; some were brushing their teeth outside on street while others were sitting out in the sun reading morning newspaper while drinking tea; radios were blaring full volume; children were playing; some women were sweeping their front porches; there were people on bikes and on auto rikshaws; some people were tending to cows and goats; there were tea stalls after every couple of houses. There was no one coordinating it all but everything was moving in perfect harmony.

Megan was amazed with this view. She watched it intently for some time and then commented, "Somebody had told me that when you go to India you start believing in the 'Order in Chaos' theory, and I guess he was right."

They drove for a few minutes and then they reached the *samosa* shop. Vikram parked the car and all three walked to the shop. The front of the shop had a slightly raised platform. On both side of the platform were two big woks - one of which had *samosas* deep frying in it, and the other one had *jalebi* deep frying in it. There were several men standing in front of the shop drinking tea in earthen bowls.

The man frying the *samosas* was Ramlal, the owner of the store. His samosas were famous all over the town. Om was a regular customer, and knew him very well. Ramlal greeted Om and Vikram whom he knew since he was a little boy. He exchanged pleasantaries with him too. He thought that Megan was Vikram's wife.

"Did you marry?" he asked Vikram.

"No, nobody has agreed to marry me yet," said Vikram smilingly.

Ramlal knew that he was kidding. A guy working in the US must be a hot commodity in the marriage market. "*Arey Sahib*, you are joking. You can get any girl you want," he said.

"Well I'll know in a few days if I can get any girl I want," said Vikram smilingly while side glancing at Megan,

Megan smiled shyly. Om noticed the sideglances of Vikram and Megan's shy smile. He suspected that something may be cooking between them two, but he ignored it.

"OK sir, what can I get for you?" asked Ramlal.

"Vickie, how many *samosas* do you think we need?"

"Well *Pappa*, we need one for *Maa*, one for Sis, one for *Dadi Maa*, two for you, two for me – and Megan how many for you?"

"Just one for me," she replied.

"Let's make two for you. That makes it 9 *samosas*," said Vikram.

Ramlal wanted to do something special for his long time customer, especially because his son had returned from US.

"*Arey Sahib*, 9 *samosas* will not be enough. I'll give you three extras, one for you, one for *chotey babu* (little master, Vikram) and one for *bitiya* (daughter Megan)," said Ramlal.

Om looked at Vikram, "What do you think Vickie?"

"The more, the better," he said.

When they arrived at the car, Om opened the passenger door and asked Megan to sit there.

"I can sit in the back," she said.

"No sit in front, you'll get a better view of the town and its morning madness," Om insisted.

This time Om decided to drive and Vikram sat in the back.

Vikram was enjoying the smell of fresh, hot *samosas.* In fact, he could see from his father's face that he was also enjoying the smell of hot and fresh samosas. He could not resist the tempetation. He lifted up the paper bag of *samosas* and asked his father, "*Pappa*, are you thinking what I'm thinking?"

Om knew what Vikram meant. "Yes, that is exactly what I am thinking, son," he replied.

Megan looked at them curiously wondering what they were talking about.

"Then, shall we do it?" asked Vikram.

"Yes, I think we should," answered Om.

"Do what?" asked Megan.

"You'll see it in a minute," said Vikram.

Om pulled over his car on the side of the street.

"Vickie, can we trust her with our secret?" he asked Vikram while sideglancing at Megan.

Vikram looked at Megan and asked, "Megan, can we trust you?"

Megan was totally confused. She had no clue what the father and son were talking about.

Vikram looked at his father and whispered, "*Pappa*, I think we can trust her."

"OK. Then you tell her," said Om.

Vikram revealed their secret to Megan, "All right, here it goes. *Maa* does not let us eat more than one *samosa*. Both *Pappa* and I love Ramlal's *somosas.* So everytime she would ask us to get *samosas*, we would buy two extra and eat one each before coming home. We have been doing it for years, and *Maa* is still clueless about it."

Megan was very amused at father and son behaving like kids. "You guys are amazing," she said.

Vikram took out one *samosa* from the bag and a napkin and offered it to Megan first.

Megan hesitated, "No thanks, I'll eat at home with everybody."

"It's your loss," he said, "*Pappa*, you take it, quick; it is very hot."

He then quickly gave the hot samosa to his father who was more than eager to take it. Vikram took out another *samosa* and a napkin for himself and they started eating. Megan could see they were clearly enjoying themselves.

Vikram looked at Megan and teased her, "Yum! Yum! They must eat this in heaven."

Megan was trying really hard to control her temptation. The smell of hot *samosa* was very tempting. She waited for a few seconds and then she could not control herself, "Ok, OK, you got me. I cannot take this torture anymore. Pass me on one too."

Vikram smiled, "That is like my girl."

He took out another *samosa* and handed it to Megan. Now all three were eating and enjoying hot *samosas.*

Om and Vikram were already done with their *samosas.* Megan was still eating hers. They wiped their faces with their napkins. Vikram looked at his father and asked in low voice, "*Pappa*, how about another one?"

While Om was tempted to eat one more but he was a little concerned.

"One more? Then we'll have to eat one more at home otherwise your mother will know that something is wrong," said Om.

Vikram encouraged him, "Oh *Pappa*, you have done it before, you can handle three *samosas*."

Om smiled and took one more *samosa* from Vikram. He looked at Megan and offered another *samosa* to Megan.

"Oh no, to keep your secret I'll have to eat one more at home. I don't think I can handle three *samosas*," she responded.

"Well, you have only a couple of minutes to change your mind," warned Vikram.

They ate the second *samosa* and Megan finished her first.

After that they all left for home.

Om parked his car in front of his house and they all walked together to go into the house. As they were about to enter the house, Megan noticed a little crum of *samosa* crust stuck near the corner of Om's upper lip. She immediately grabbed his hand and stopped him from opening the door. "*Pappa*," she almost screamed.

They froze wondering why she stopped them. She looked at Om and asked, "Can I also call you *Pappa*?"

"Is that why you stopped us?" Vikram asked her.

Om was emotionally touched by Megan referring to him as "*Pappa*". He slowly approached Megan and hugged her gently. "Sure, my child," he told her. Meanwhile, Vikram was quite thrilled to see that Megan just scored a lot of points with his father.

Megan then pointed to the crum stuck on Om's upper lip. He wiped his face with his hand.

"Oh my God, we have to remove all evidence of the crime," he said.

The crum was still there. Megan removed the crum from her finger and then wiped Om's lips with her napkin. She still had the napkin in her hand as they were about to enter the house.

Om was emotionally moved, first that Megan addressed him as *Pappa*, and second that she removed the crum with her fingers. He felt as if Megan was his own daughter.

Megan was still holding the oil stained napkin in her hand. Vikram immediately stopped Megan and pointed to the napkin in her hand. "Megan, crime scene evidence," he whispered to her.

"Where?" she wondered.

"In your hand," he pointed to the napkin in her hand.

She looked around for a place to throw it.

Vikram took her napkin, looked around and could not find any safe place to throw it.

Meanwhile, Maya heard Om's car pull in and wondered what was taking them so long to come in. Maya opened the door. As soon as Maya opened the door, Vilram quickly hid the napkin and put it in his pocket.

"What is taking you guys so long?" she asked, "I heard the car pull in five minutes ago."

Om quickly made up an excuse, "Oh, Vickie was showing Megan our garden."

Vikram and Megan handed over the *samosa* and *jalebi* bags to Maya. She did not suspect anything.

They all followed Maya to the breakfast table. While walking behind her, Vikram quietly did thumbs up signal to Om and they secretly did high five and smiled for flawless execution of their act. Megan thoroughly enjoyed father and son's child like behavior.

Natasha and *Dadi Maa* were already sitting there. Maya removed *samosa* and *jalebi* from the bags and placed them on two empty plates.

"So, Megan what did you think of the morning chaos in this town?" Maya asked.

"Oh, I thoroughly enjoyed it. It looked very lively," answered Megan.

"Because you don't have to deal with this everyday," jested Om.

Megan smiled, looked at Om and Maya, and continued, "I would like to say one more thing – I've been here with you all only for few hours, but within this short time I feel like I know you all for years."

"I also feel that you are part of this family," Maya reciprocated.

Vikram and Natasha did a secret thumps up. It appeared that Maya had developed a liking for Megan.

Megan continued, "I've never seen such a fun loving family. I feel fortunate to have an opportunity to spend this time with you all."

As Megan stopped, Maya got up and hugged her.

"Truly a great speech" joked Vikram while leading an applause for her. Natasha, *Dadi Maa* and Om joined him.

"Vikram, how come you are not attacking *samosas*. Normally you and your *Pappa* pounce on *samosas* like wild eagles," wondered Maya.

Om looked at Vikram and challenged him, "Son, you are at least two inches taller than me. You can handle a couple of *somosas*."

Vikram took the plate and put one *samosa* in Om's plate and one on Megan's plate.

Om and Vikram ate their *samosas* very slowly. Maya looked at Vikram and wondered, "Are the *samosas* not good?"

"They are fine, Maa," he answered.

Dadi Maa chimed in, "Looks like the pizzas and spaggetti have killed your liking for *samosas* but I guess that is good because deep fried stuff is not very healthy for you."

Vikram pretended to agree with his grand mother. "Yes *Dadi Maa*, I've been trying to avoid deep fried food," he said.

"I avoid deep fried food too," Om butted in.

Maya cut him off, "Yes sure. You are not attacking *samosa* right now perhaps because Vickie started watching his food."

Again, Om, Vikram and Megan tried to control their smile.

"While you guys set examples for each other, I'm eating it before it gets cold," said Natasha while biting into a hot samosa.

Natasha continued, "Ok, what is the plan for the rest of the day?"

Maya suggested that they take Megan out for sightseeing.

"No, I've a better idea," Natasha jumped in, "I think Megan should go out shopping with us."

"I think you four ladies should go shopping. I am going to hang around with my son and watch cricket game between India and England," said Om.

Vikram jumped with happiness, "There is a game today? I want to watch it. I haven't watched cricket in such a long time."

"OK, we girls are going shopping. Let's go," announced Maya.

She then turned toward them, "Since both of you are staying back, make sure that you put all the leftovers away, wash the dishes, and clean the breakfast table."

Om looked at Vikram and asked him, "Vickie, do you still want to stay home?"

"Oh, don't worry *Pappa*; we'll finish all this work in no time," he said confidently, "We'll show them that it's really no work at all."

She muttered, "I've this feeling that nothing will be done."

Om heard her mutter. He stood up like a great statesman and told his wife, "My dear, remember what great american president John F. Kennedy said? He said, 'Ask not what your hasband can do for you, ask what you can do for your husband'."

The girls all burst into laughter while Vikram and his dad secretely high-fived.

As soon as they left, Vikram decided to finish the cleaning. But Om wanted to watch the cricket game on TV.

"Vikram let's put all the dishes in the sink and soak them in water," suggested Om, "It'll be easier to clean them when they are already soaked."

"That is a good idea," Vikram quickly agreed.

Vikram's mind was occupied with how he was going to tell his parents about what was cooking between him and Megan. He was confident that Om would have no problem with him marrying Megan, but he was not too sure about his mother. He wanted to tell Om about it but before that he decided to check with his sister to see what she thought.

After they piled up the dishes in the sink, Vikram proceeded to the bathroom to find a quiet place to call Natasha.

"Where are you going?" asked Om.

"I'm going to the bathroom," he replieed.

Vikram closed the bathroom door and called Natasha.

Vikram whispered into the phone, "Sis, this is me, but if *Maa* is near you, say after how many minutes I should call you back and say that it was a wrong number, and then hang up."

Natasha was driving. She realized that *Maa* could overhear their conversation. Her mind was working overtime. She quickly thought of what to say. She pretended to be irritated with the call – "Every ten minutes I get a prank call," she said while angrily turning the phone off. She put her phone on the cup holder in her car.

"Who was it?" Maya asked.

"It was some prank call," said Natasha.

Vikram got the signal to call her back in ten minutes. He came back to where Om was watching cricket.

"Did I miss anything?" he asked.

"India won the toss and they just started batting. It's 5 runs for no wicket," reported Om.

Meanwhile Natasha parked her car. She quickly cooked up an excuse to get away from Maya so she could find out why Vikram called her. Natasha stealthily left her cellphone under a magazine in her car.

All four of them walked to the shopping mall. When they reached the Mall entrance, Natasha pretended to look for her phone. Obviously, she could not find it because it was in the car.

"Where is my cellphone?" she panicked.

Maya was worried too. She asked her to look into her purse. Natasha pretended to be looking into her purse again.

"Let me call your cellphone," suggested Maya, "see if it rings."

She called her phone. Obviously there was no sound.

"I may have left it in the car," Natasha said while running to the parking lot, "You guys wait here. I'll be right back."

She quickly ran to her car, picked up her phone and called Vikram. He was sitting with Om watching cricket match. He suspected that it must be Natasha. He answered the phone while walking away from the TV room.

"*Bhaiyaa*, it's me. What's up?" she asked.

"I just thought that since I'm alone with *Pappa*, shall I feel him out about Megan?" he asked.

Natasha pondered for a second, "I think it'll be good idea to bring *Pappa* on board. You should definitely go for it. I got to run now otherwise *Maa* would wonder where I was. I'll get a report from you later. OK bye."

Natasha quickly walked and joined Maya and Megan.

"Did you find it?" asked Maya.

"Yes it was right there," she said.

Maya was relieved. "I am glad you remembered it just in time otherwise these days people break into cars just to steal phones," she said.

After talking to Natasha, Vikram joined Om.

"Who was it?" asked Om.

"It was Natasha asking me if I wanted her to buy anything," he said.

Vikram sat there wondering how he was going to muster the courage to tell Om about Megan. Then finally he thought of a way.

"*Pappa*, how did you and *Maa* meet?" he asked.

"Why do you want to know that?" asked Om wondering why all of a sudden Vikram wanted to know that.

"I'm just curious," said Vikram.

"Well it was all arranged by our family," he replied.

"So your family told you to marry some stranger and you agreed?" asked Vikram.

"No, my family found this stranger, but the decision to marry that stranger was mostly mine," he explained.

"Can you walk me through the whole process?" asked Vikram.

"Why do you want to know this?" asked Om.

"I'll tell you in a second," replied Vikram.

Om took his reading glasses off and put it on the side table, took a deep a breath, and gazed toward the ceiling for a few moments. "Oh, it's a long process," he tried to summarize it for him, "The boy' and girl's families do a lot of background research on each other's family, education, even their medical histories."

Vikram interrupted, "Medical histories? Isn't that supposed to be private information?"

"Yes, it's but if you dig hard enough you can find out if there are any serious issues," he said, "They also try to find out if there are any skeletons in their closets. And it's only after both parties pass through this rigorous screening, do the boy and girl get a chance to meet."

Vikram frowned at this explaination and commented, "This seems so mechanical – like buying a car or something."

"Well, think of it as applying for a job in a company called the 'Married Life'," explained Om, "Compared to the regular job hunt, there are two major differences here. No. 1 - both boy and girl are employers and employees at the same time, and No 2. - there are no negotiations on employment package, no hiring bonuses etc. – what you see is what you get – although in some strange cases the boy's family may demand a hefty hiring bonus in the form of a dowry."

Vikram was looking for the right opportunity to bring in Megan's name in this discussion. "You know in US, they find this process to be really strange," he said.

Om concurred with him, "You are right. In fact, the new generation in India considers this process strange." He contunued, "Well; different times call for different approaches to do things. In my days, interactions between girls and boys were limited, and thus the parent's connection in finding mates was perhaps the best way. But now such traditions are rapidly fading because of the obvious reasons."

Vikram saw the opening here, "So, today if you were a young man, you would choose your mate youself?"

"What do you mean if I was a young man? I am a young man," Om joked.

"*Pappa*, I meant if you were in the market for marriage," said Vikram smilingly.

Om again took a deep breath and tried to find the real reason behind this conversation. "Well, son let's not worry about what I would have done, tell me what you want to do?" he asked, "Do you want to be a lazy man and expect us to find you a bride or you'll be responsible enough to do this important job yourself?"

Vikram decided this to be right opening to tell him about Megan.

"*Pappa*, I'm not lazy anymore," he blurted it out.

Om was not too sure what that meant. He asked, "That means you are going to find a bride for yourself, or have you already found one?"

Vikram hesitated while Om anxiously looked at him for an answer.

Vikram called upon all of his faculties to cooperate. This was not the time to shy away, to stammer, or to vascillate. He looked at his father and declared, "*Pappa*, I've already found one." Before Om could react, he added, "but everything is pending until you and *Maa* approve."

Om was ecstatic. He believed he knew who the girl was. He had noticed how Vikram had been interacting with Megan - the prolonged eye contact at many occasions, their fondness for each other – it all started to add up. Megan must be the girl. He smiled and said to Vikram, "Don't tell me who she is. Let me guess."

Vikram was sure that his father will never guess it right because they all had been acting their parts so well.

Om closed his eyes and pretended to be in deep thought.

"My sixth sense tells me that the girl in question is Megan, am I right?" he asked.

Vikram was blown away. "*Pappa*, how did you know that?" asked Vikram with his eyes wide open.

"Son, remember when you were 11 years old and one day you skipped school and were playing soccer instead of being in your classes and your clothes were all muddy?"

"Yes, I remember that," he said.

Om continued, "And when I asked you why your clothes were dirty, you never said a word about soccer or about missing your class. You told us that you tripped on a dirt field."

"I remember that too," said Vikram.

"Who was the one who knew that you were hiding something?" asked Om.

"It was you," he admitted.

Om continued, "One of the bonuses of being a teacher is that this job sharpens your sixth sense of reading faces. I hear all kinds of creative excuses from students on why they did poorly in a test, or why they could not turn in their homework in time. So son, you can give an Oscar winning acting performance, but your *Pappa* can see right through you."

"So tell me how long you have known Megan?" Om asked.

Vikram smiled and taunted him, "*Pappa*, didn't you just say that you knew everything?"

"Let's not act smart here," Om cautioned him, "didn't you just say that everything is pending until our approval? I hope you want my approval, don't you?"

Vikram quickly realized that he had to have his father on his side, "Oh yes *Pappa*. I definitely want your approval. I've known Megan for the last two years."

"So this act that Megan is working with Natasha is all cowdung?" Om asked.

"Yes, and by the way, in the US they call it 'horseshit,' not cowdung," said Vikram.

"It doesn't matter what they call it in the US. They are both crap," replied Om.

They both laughed.

"You know, I like the girl. Again my sixth sense tells me that she is a great human being," said Om, "But you know my son, you have a problem."

Vikram curiously looked on.

"Your problem is her dark skin," he warned, "Your mother is going to have a fit."

"So, how do we solve this problem?" asked Vikram.

"Tell me how long Megan is going to be in India?" asked Om.

"We are flying back together after two weeks," answered Vikram

Om was relieved to hear that. "That means we have some time. I'll have to think about it," he said, "But the fact that Megan is spending some time with us is a great thing. It'll help Megan and Maya bond."

"Let's continue thinking how we want to bring your mother on board," suggested Om, "Meanwhile let's see what is going on in the cricket game."

They got quite engrossed in cricket match. They watched the entire match for the full 4 hours.

Then suddenly they heard the door bell.

Vikram looked at the clock. It was almost evening time, and when he looked out the window, the girls had returned. He panicked. The dishes had not been done. He turned toward his father, "*Pappa*, the dishes!"

Om was also startled seeing Vikram's sudden panic. "What dishes?" he asked.

Vikram spoke rapidly in low voice, "The dishes, we did not do the dishes."

As soon as Om realized what Vikram was saying, he bolted from his seat. "Son, you handle the situation, I am out of here," said Om while running upstairs to his bedroom.

Vikram opened the door. As soon as Maya walked in, she noticed the dirty breakfast table and the dishes.

"As I expected, these guys have not done anything," she said angrily, "Vikram, where is your *Pappa*?"

At the same time Om slowly walked out of his room pretending to be just woken up by the noise. He took a big yawn.

"Oh, you guys are already back? What time is it?" he said while rubbing his eyes.

"It is 4 O'Clock," said Maya.

Om pretended to be in shock, "Oh my goodnesss. Vickie, why didn't you wake me up? I had told you that we'll clean up after I take a little nap."

Vikram shook his head and looked at his father admiringly about the trick that he just pulled on him.

Natasha came to her father's rescue, "Oh don't worry *Maa*; we'll clean up."

"I can help if you want," Vikram offered.

Natasha looked at him suscipiciously, "Are you sure you want to help rather than watch cricket."

"Are you giving me a choice?" he asked.

"OK brother, you can continue watching cricket. I'll do the dishes. But remember, you owe me one," she said.

"I owe you more than one, my sweet sister," said Vikram

Vikram looked at his father, "*Pappa*, you missed a great cricket match. Do you want to watch now or continue sleeping… like you were?"

CHAPTER XXVIII

Utter Joy

Dadi Maa was ready to go back to her home, and Vikram volunteerd to drive her. Megan decided to come with them too. Natasha proposed that when they returned, they would all go to a movie.

Dadi Maa's house was about 10 minutes drive. They both returned in half an hour. Natasha was already waiting for them.

"Which movie are we going to go?" asked Vikram.

"I think Megan will like Devdas," proposed Natasha, "It's a good love story and has some good dance numbers."

"Natasha! Which show you guys are planning to go?" asked Maya.

"I was thinking of the 11 O'Clock show," she answered.

Maya looked at the clock. "Then you guys don't have much time," she pointed out, "You better get ready soon."

Natasha took Megan to her room to dress her up.

Vikram looked at his watch. "You ladies have only five minutes to get ready," he warned.

"Five minutes for two girls to dress up? You must be kidding," said Natasha, "We'll try to be out in 15 minutes."

"Then I'll have to drive like a maniac to get to the movie in time," he warned.

"Don't worry, I'll drive," she said, "I can reach there in time."

Vikram went to his room to get ready. He came out in jeans and shirt and sat on a sofa and watched TV. He looked at his watch and worried.

After several minutes, both Natasha and Megan came out and they both looked stunningly beautiful in salwar kurta. "Oh look at you girls.

Instead of watching movies, people are going to watch you guys," said Vikram while looking at them flirtatiously, "You know, you guys are really lucky."

"Why?" asked Megan while Natasha looked on curiously.

"If looking stunningly beautiful was against the law, both of you would be in jail."

They both blushed. "Are we overdressed?" asked Natasha.

"No, No, you're not overdressed, you guys look just knock out gorgeous," he said.

After they left, Maya was in a good mood seeing how happy her children were. She sat next to Om on the sofa.

"Om, do you want some coffee?" she asked.

"Yes sure, but let me make it for you," he proposed as he left for the kitchen.

He brought two cups of coffee to the family room where Maya was sitting. Maya's eyes were a little damp.

"Are you ok?" he asked.

She nodded quietly while taking the coffee cup from him. He sat next to her and waited for her response. She wiped her eyes. "You know, I feel so happy seeing our kids laughing and enjoying their life. But then when I think about Natasha, I feel sad," she revealed.

"Why do you feel sad about Natasha?" he wondered.

She explained, "Look at Vickie. He is good looking, smart, has an excellent career and is of light skin. But my poor Natasha, she has everything, but why did God give her dark skin?"

Om shook his head in frustration and murmured, "Here we go again."

She continued, "Mr. Mathur's son was a good match for her but perhaps I destroyed everything. I should never have tried to hide Natasha's skin color. That was a complete deception. If I had presented her the way she was, perhaps outcome would have been different. I don't know what I was thinking."

He comforted her, "Let it go, Maya. It was my mistake too. I should have told you about switching Natasha's pictures before mailing them to Mr. Mathur."

She was still choked up, "No, you did the right thing by sending them the right pictures. It was me who was not thinking straight."

She continued, "I'll never forgive myself. If I had been honest about Natasha's skin color perhaps they would have accepted Natasha."

As soon as he heard this he got a little upset. He removed his hand from Maya's shoulders. "Maya, you sound desparate, you sound like you are begging for a groom," said Om with his voice a little raised, "From what

I hear from you it seems that you are not sorry for being deceptive, instead you are sorry that your deception may have changed Mathur's decision. How many times do I've to remind you that this kind of behavior will have a detrimental effect on Natasha?"

She started to wail now, "Now you can say whatever you want."

At this point Om tried another angle. "Let me ask you something. What if Megan wanted to marry Vickie? How will you feel?" he asked.

She immediately stopped crying. She looked at Om strangely wondering how he could even pose such a bizarre question.

"There are a lot of girls that would want to marry him. He is fair skinned, good looking boy. But that does not mean that I've to entertain all of them," she said with a little arrogance in her voice.

He tweaked her more, "What if Vickie also wanted to marry Megan?"

She was a little agitated with even the thought of Vikram and Megan marrying.

"Why on earth would he want that? Are there no light skin girls left in the world?" she said disdainfully.

Maya's response made him cringe, but he tried to keep calm and repeated his question, "What if Vickie also wanted to marry Megan?"

"He is my son. I know he will never do that," said Maya, still stalling to answer his question.

Om did not give up. He persisted, "What if Vickie also wanted to marry Megan?"

"He is grown up. He can do whatever he wants. Who am I to say anything?" she responded angrily.

He pushed on, "You did not answer my question. I asked how you'll feel."

She wiped tears of her face and said, "It's not how I'll feel. All our family and friends are going to be totally shocked if Vikram decides to marry a black girl. And besides, black culture and our culture are very different. It is ok for her to spend a few days with us, but spending life together is unthinkable."

He was outraged with her response, "Black culture? Megan is born and raised in US. And you know what? If Megan was white, then the cultural differences would not have been an issue, because then your family and friends will feel proud of Vikram's 'catch.' It is not she; it is skin that she is in, isn't it? And when others do this to your own daugher, you wonder why. This is the height of hypocracy."

She was now worried about what he said about Vikram and Megan. Was something cooking between them? Her expressions changed from being sad to panic. She asked, "Is something going on between Vickie and Megan?"

"Now you have something else to worry about," he scoffed.

"Tell me, please," she insisted.

Seeing that she did not respond well to the hypothetical Vikram-Megan union, he decided to delay telling her the truth. "That was just a hypothetical question," he said.

She was relaxed now. Meanwhile the telephone rang.

"You answer the phone. I am not in a mood to talk to anybody right now," she told him.

He went to his bedroom upstaires to receive the call. It was Mr. Mathur on the phone.

"Mr. Mathur, how are you?"

"I was calling to find out what Natasha thought about Ashok," said Mr. Mathur, "I spoke to Ashok and he is determined to steal your daughter from you."

Om was thrilled to hear this news. He always believed that Ashok was an excellent match for his daughter.

"Oh that is wonderful news," he answered, "I've not talked to Natasha about Ashok. My son is visiting from the US, and they have gone to a movie."

Mr. Mathur was aware of the frequent phone and email conversations between Ashok and Natasha. He knew that they had developed a strong adoration for each other. Om and Maya knew nothing about it.

"You have given her an excellent upbringing. I think she is a wonderful girl," said Mr. Mathur, "Well, you can talk to Natasha about it but I know her answer."

"What do you mean?" asked Om.

Mr. Mathur realized that perhaps Om did not know about the email and telephonic romance between them. "Mr. Srivastava, this is 20th century," said Mr. Mathur, "Children, these days, are much smarter than what we were in our times. I don't know if you knew that Natasha and Ashok have been chatting regularly and they have developed a great fondness for each other."

Om was pleasantly surprised, "Oh really? I had no clue about it."

"Yes, Ashok told us all about it," said Mr. Mathur, "He is hoping that Mrs. Srivastava and you would consider him worthy enough for Natasha."

Om was humbled by his gesture, "That is very kind of you to say that. We think that Ashok is a nice young man."

"So shall I consider this as yes from you?" asked Mr. Mathur.

"It's a resounding yes from me. Let me talk to Natasha and I'll get back to you soon," Om answered.

"I'll be anxiously waiting to hear from you," said Mr. Mathur, "And also, Ashok is here for only two weeks. If everything works out, we would like to arrange the marriage within two weeks."

"I think that will be a great idea," Om responded jubiliantly, "Vikram can then also attend their wedding."

Om was delighted that Maya will be thrilled when she learned about this news. He decided to capitalize on this news and use it to convince Maya about Vikram and Megan. He walked to the family room trying to hide his happiness. Maya was still sitting in the living room in a kind of subdued mood. "Who was it?" she asked.

"A friend of mine," he said.

Then there was again a dead silence in the room for several seconds. Om was trying hard to hide his emotions.

"Maya, when I asked you that hypothetical question about Vikram and Megan…," he said and watched for changing expressions on Maya's face.

Maya immediately looked up to Om with curiosity. "Yes?" she asked.

Om paused again a little while Maya looked at him curiously with worried look.

With a straight face, he revealed, "It was not a hypothetical question."

Maya's mood changed suddenly. Her eyes widened. Her voice changed from being subdued to alarm. "What do you mean? It can't be true," she panicked.

He revealed more, "Vikram and Megan love each other."

"Nonsense!" she exploded, "How can they love each other? He has known her only for two days."

"No, they have known each other for the last two years," Om shared more details, "In fact they came to India together to attend our anniversary."

Maya was very agitated now. "What?" she screamed, "How do you know all this?"

"Vikram told me all about it," he divulged.

Maya could not stand it anymore. "Why am I always the last person to learn about these things?" she roared.

"Because your children know how you feel about dark skin color," he said.

She could not control her anguish and frustration. She started to sob again, "Let him do whatever he wants. Who am I to stop him? If he wanted to marry a dark girl, he could have gotten one here in India, why did he have to bring one from the US."

With that she stomped off to her bedroom. Om followed her and caught up with her in the bedroom. "Look at your hypocracy! You don't want to give your son to a dark skinned girl, but you expect others to see Natasha's quailities, not her dark skin," he said.

Maya hid her head in her hands and bent down and sobbed.

After a few seconds, Om tried to calm her down, "Maya, Megan is a beautiful and bright girl. You should feel happy that Vickie has found somebody he likes."

Maya sat dazed for few more seconds. Then she uncovered her face and raised her head. Her eyes were all wet. She wiped her face with her *sari*. "I had so many dreams for him. But, does he care about my dreams?" she said sobbingly.

"And, what about his dreams?" he interjected, "How can you be so selfish to expect him to care about your dreams while you are destroying his dreams?"

She stayed quiet but still visibly distraught.

He continued, "And you must mark my words. If you prevent him from marrying the girl of his choice, you'll lose your son."

She was still quiet with her head down.

He added, "If you force him using your motherly powers, he may succumb to it because that is how we have raised him, but he will never forgive you for the rest of his life."

She started to understand what he had been telling her. She could not bear the thought of losing her son or making him unhappy. She tried to accept the situation, "You are right. It's hypocritical on my part. I should feel happy about it otherwise I am going to lose my children. You are right, as much as I know about Megan, I like everything about her."

She started to sob again with tears rolling down her eyes. He tried to comfort Maya by rubbing her back. Maya paused for a second and then spoke again, "Don't worry, these are tears of joy." He continued to rub her back.

"I know I am wrong. I was wrong when I doctored Natasha's pictures and I was wrong when I tried to hide Natasha's skin with makeup," she admitted.

Om comforted her, "Let's forget about that."

She continued, "I know deep down that my daughter is very beautiful, very talented and whoever marries her will be a very lucky man."

He concurred, "You are absolutely right, Maya. And please stop worrying about Natasha. She'll do just fine."

She held his hands, looked into his eyes and said, "Om, can I ask you for a favor?"

"Sure, now since you have come back to your senses, anything for you," he answered.

"Will you please not tell Vickie that I know about him and Megan? He has played so many tricks on me; let me play one on him too," she said.

"What trick?" he asked.

"Don't worry, let me deal with it myself and try to win my children back, so next time they are not afraid to share their feelings with me," she told him.

She was still not completely over the initial shock of the relationship between Vikram and Megan, and on top of that, her lingering concern was that nothing was yet settled for her daughter. She wanted to see both of her children happy.

Om hadn't yet told her about Mr. Mathur's call. He could see mixed emotions on her face. He knew that she would be overjoyed when she heard about it. He had been trying hard to keep a straight face since he talked to Mr. Mathur. He could not keep it any longer. Moreover, he was anxious to see the utter joy on her face when she heard the news. He slowly approached her keeping a grim face one last time. "Maya, I am carrying another secret for the last 10 minutes," he said.

Maya had already had enough shocks for the day. She could not take it anymore. Her face immediately tightened in anticipation of another shocker. She looked at him, "Om, please don't torture me any more. What is it?"

Om came closer to Maya and held her tight. He was unable to control his emotions. His eyes dampened. As soon as she saw Om's wet eyes, she forgot her own anguish.

"Please tell me. What is it?" she begged him.

"Our daughter is not going to be with us for much longer," said Om with teary eyes.

Maya was extremely worried now. She pulled away from him and screamed, "Om, you are going to give me a heart attack. Please tell me what is going on."

While his eyes still wet, he smiled. "You know who the friend was who called me a few minutes ago?" he asked.

Not knowing what he was saying, she was about to explode, "Who was it?"

"It was Mr. Mathur," he said.

"So what did he say?" she burst in.

Om was almost sobbing with the thought that his daughter is going to be gone soon.

"They want to take our daughter away from us," he revealed.

She could not believe what she just heard. Her facial expressions quickly changed from worried to total disbelief to shear ecstacy. She stuttered, "You mean......"

He interrupted her, "Yes, they and their son are in love with our daughter. And they want to finalize the marriage if Natasha agrees."

Now she was really escatic. Her eyes dampened again, but this time the dampness was the result of her shear joy. She ran to him and hugged him tight. It took several seconds for her to collect herself. She let go of him, looked toward heavens, folded her hands and thanked God.

Recalling that Om was in a habit of playing tricks on her, she was afraid that this may be another of his jokes. She turned toward him, "Om, please tell me that you are not playing with me. Because if you are, I'll never forgive you for this cruel joke."

"No my dear, this is what Mr. Mathur said," he said, "And you know one more thing? Mr Mathur wants to do the wedding within two weeks."

Maya could not contain her joy. She wanted to know every word Mr. Mathur said to make sure that there are no surprises.

"What did you tell him?" she asked.

"I told him that I'll call him back after I talked to you."

While still in the fantasy land, she began to digest the news. She was now in more control of herself. "But we should ask Natasha first before proceeding any further," she proposed.

He agreed. He chose not to tell Maya about the regular chats between Natasha and Ashok.

"What do you think Natasha would say?" she asked him.

"I don't know. We'll find out as soon as she returns," he replied.

CHAPTER XXIX

An Outdoor Experience

"So Megan, what did you think of the movie?" asked Vikram while driving back, "Did you understand it?"

"Oh yes, I may not have understood every conversation but I understood the story," she responded, "The story seemed like a fairy tale but the dances were beautiful."

"Most Indian movies are all about dances and songs," said Natasha.

Megan had already heard about the big movie industry in India. She asked, "So the lead actor in this movie is a big star in India, isn't he?"

"He is really a big star," said Natasha.

"What is his name?" she asked.

Natasha burst into laughter and said, "OH, I love it. I know somebody who does not know Shah Rukh Khan."

Megan tried to repeat his name in her American accent. They all laughed at Megan's attempt. They chatted and laughed while driving. They passed by a *chaat* vendor on the side of the street. Natasha tapped on Vikram's shoulders, "*Bhaiyya*, let's try some *chaat*. I bet Megan has never tried that."

"What is *chaat*?" asked Megan.

Natasha explained, "*Chaat* means lick. *Chaat* is also a special type of snack that tastes sooo good that you can't stop licking your fingers. That is why it's called *chaat*"

"OK, let's introduce Megan to *chaat*," said Vikram.

He pulled over to a parking space near the vendor. They all started to walk over to the vendor. There were several people eating *chaat* on the side of the street near the vender. It reminded her of hot dog venders often found near major intersections.

"Sis, what should we order?" he asked.

"*Dahi Bada* at this place is famous. Let's get that," she suggested.

Vikram placed three orders of *Dahi Bada*. He brought the orders near his car where Megan and Natasha stood. Megan looked at the crooked looking bowls containing *Dahi Bada* and a flat wooden spoon that looked more like a tongue depresser. "What is it?" she asked.

"This is a 'high tech' bowl made with some kind of leaves. They call it *dona*," answered Vikram jokingly.

"Oh, that is amazing," said Megan.

"And you know the interesting thing about these?" continued Natasha, "After you use them, you throw them. It comes from the nature and goes back to the nature without leaving any carbon footprints."

Using her flat wooden spoon, Megan ate slowly to get the taste first, but as soon as she got used to its strong spicy flavor, she enjoyed it, "This is really good. The sauce has a lot of flavor. I wonder why they don't sell these things in the US."

"They do sell it in big cities like New York and Chicago," said Vikram, "but it may not be as authentic and they may not serve it in *dona*."

"I'm going to take two carryout orders of *Dahi Bada* for *Maa* and *Pappa* too," he suggested.

"Yes, that is good idea," Natasha agreed with a smile.

CHAPTER XXX

Getting Even

Maya was at home and impatiently waiting for them to return so she could break the great news to Natasha. She looked at the clock. She was getting restless. "The movie finished at 2:30. Where are these guys?" she murmured.

"The traffic in this town can sometimes be a total nightmare. Why don't you call them?" suggested Om.

She called Natasha. As soon as Natasha's phone rang she was already at the front door. It was Maya calling. Natasha signaled everybody to be quiet and tiptoed quietly in the house.

Natasha answered while entering her house. Maya stood with her back facing the main door. So she did not see them entering. Om could see them entering. But Natasha signaled him also to be quiet. Everybody was quietly smiling.

"Betey, where are you?" asked Maya.

"We are not too far," responded Natasha.

"When will you be coming home?"

"Soon"

"What do you mean soon?"

Natasha came directly behind her mother and screams, "Soon means soon soon soon."

Maya was startled with the noise. She turned around and found all of them laughing, "Oh you guys have to trick me on everything. Where were you?"

"We decided to try some *Dahi Bada's*, and we have brought some for you too."

Om got excited about the mention of *Dahi Bada*, "Oh, *Dahi Bada*, yum, yum, yum."

"Why don't you guys wash your faces and use the bathroom if you have to. I'll make some coffee," said Maya.

Vikram and Megan left for their respective rooms. Natasha went to the kitchen to transfer *Dahi Bada* into regular bowls.

Maya and Om were now alone in the room.

"Do you want to talk to Natasha?" she whispered into Om's ears.

Om whispered back, "Do you want me to?"

"Yes. You do it because I am just too excited," she said.

They both came to the kitchen where Natasha was still there.

Om knew that Natasha and Ashok already liked each other. Thus, he decided not to mince words and come straight to the point.

"Betey, Natasha. Mr. Mathur is asking for your hand for their son Ashok. What do you think about him?" he asked.

Through her conversation with Ashok, Natasha already knew that Mr. Mathur was going to call. She acted startled by this direct question. She knew that her parents liked Ashok.

"What do you guys think about him?" she said blushingly with a little smile.

He joked, "I don't think there is any boy in this world who is good enough for my daughter."

Natasha smiled and hugged Om, "Thank you, *Pappa*."

Om continued, "But based on my research, I think Ashok comes pretty close."

"You did research on him?" she wondered.

"Yes, I did," he said, "Before I invited Mathurs to our house I already did a great deal of investigation on Ashok. I talked to his professors, all his bosses where he worked. I would not have invited them to our house if he did not meet my tough standards. So he has a green signal from me."

Om and Maya were quietly waiting for Natasha's response. It was clear that everybody approved of Ashok. To make her parents feel better, Natasha said, "I leave everything to your judgement. If you think this is what I should do, I'll do that."

He wanted to make sure that his daughter was completely satisfied. "No *betey*, don't do it because we want it," he said, "I am sure there are certain qualities you want in your life partner which perhaps I am not able to see."

Natasha paused and spoke shyly, "I like him."

Om then spoke in raised voice as if he is announcing to the world, "OK, then my daughter is getting married to Ashok."

Maya was very happy. Natasha smiled and hugged her parents.

Meanwhile, Vikram walked into the kitchen. "Why is she getting hugs?" he asked.

"Because somebody is getting married," told Maya.

"Who?" he asked.

"Your sister," she said.

Vikram already knew about her telephonic affair with Ashok, but he acted surprised, "Oh really? Sis, you never told me."

Natasha looked at him and smiled.

Maya then asked Vikram's opinion whether Natasha should marry Ashok. Vikram put on a serious face, "Natasha can do whatever she wants, but I wouldn't marry him."

Natasha gave him a strange look. Om and Maya were worried that there may be something that Vikram did not like about Ashok.

"Why, you don't like him?" asked Maya worriedly.

He smiled. "*Maa*, it does not matter whether I like him or not. I cannot marry him? I'm a man," he said.

They all burst into laughter.

Vikram decided to make use of this happy moment and feel her mother out about Megan. "OK *Maa*, Natasha is taken care of now. Who is going to find a bride for me?" he asked.

Maya was ready for him. She had her own plans to get even with him. She looked at him lovingly and said, "Don't you worry my son, I've a perfect girl for you in mind."

At this point Megan walked into the kitchen. Simultaneously, Vikram looked at Om and gave him a perplexed look. He wondered "Which girl does *Maa* have in mind for me? Did *Pappa* already tell her about Megan?"

Om could see the worried look on his face. He signaled him to relax.

Maya decided to let Vikram's imagination wander around for a while. She turned to Megan. "Megan, we have good news to tell you. Natasha will be getting married soon," she said.

"Oh really? To Ashok?" she blurted it out.

Maya rolled her eyes, "So you know everything?"

Megan realized that she might have spilled the beans again. She tried to quickly recover, "Natasha told me briefly about him while we were driving."

"Ok, let's celebrate tonight," Om butted in, "Son, do you remember how Srivastavas celebrates their great moments?"

Like an obedient soldier, he responded, "Yes Your Highness! It has been the tradition of Srivastava family to celebrate their great moments by consuming a large amount of alcohol."

Om spoke in a king like voice while Maya, Natasha and Megan smiled and watched them, "That is right my son. You should always remember and follow your family traditions."

Vikram added, "And what a coincidence *Pappa*, Megan told us that her family has exactly the same tradition."

Om spoke again in a king like voice, "Remember my son, great minds think alike."

"That is right *Pappa*," he concurred.

Meanwhile Maya was so happy that she decided to let these guys do anything they wanted. "OK, I'll cook something to go with the drinks," she offered.

Om again spoke in a king like voice, "Son, what is the other tradition of Srivastava family?"

"Your Highness! When we celebrate, we don't count calories while consuming alcohol and we order food from outside," he announced.

Maya was amused to see them behave like this. She was so happy that she would let these guys do anything they wanted. "Ok, go and order whatever you want," she said.

Om asked Vikram to order *kababs, cheese pokora* and whatever else anybody wanted. Then he went to his drink's cabinet to check his inventory of wines.

"Natasha, please go and set up the dinner table. We are all going to get wasted tonight," declared Maya.

Vikram, Om and Natasha left to do their respective chores. At that point, Megan and Maya were alone in the kitchen.

Megan also prepared to leave to her room. But before she left she turned toward Maya. "Can I also call you *Maa*?" she asked Maya.

Maya immediately hugged her. "Sure my child," she said lovingly.

"Thank you. OK *Maa*, is there anything I can do?" asked Megan.

Maya wanted to talk to Megan about something else in private. This was the perfect moment when they were alone.

"Yes, you can do a lot of things for me. But first you can answer my questions," asked Maya.

"What is it, *Maa*?" asked Megan

"Oh, it sounds so good when you call me *Maa*," she said.

They both smiled.

"You may find it strange what I am going to tell you," said Maya.

She looked at Maya with curiosity.

"In your culture boys and girls choose their own partners, isn't it?" she asked.

"Yes," she answered.

"They spend time together to know each other before they decide to marry?" Maya asked again.

Megan did not know where Maya was headed.

"Yes," she replied.

"I would like Vickie to find somebody whom he likes," said Maya.

Maya paused a little and then continued, "Since Vickie became a young man, I've been fantasizing about who his bride would be; what she'll look like, etc. etc. And now looking at you, I feel you are the girl of my fantasies. I also know that not all fantasies come true, so if you have any other plans I'll will be disappointed but I'll understand."

Megan was speechless. What she had heard about Maya was not true at all. She blushed and decided that she could not lie about their relationship anymore. She took a deep breath and revealed, "Well *Maa*, I've to tell you the truth now. Vickie asked me to play along in this act that he planned, but I cannot deceive you anymore. The truth is that Vickie and I've known each other for the last two years."

Maya smiled. "Do you like him?" she asked.

"All I can say is that I'm fortunate to have met a family like yours. I would be very happy if I can find somebody like Vickie," said Megan.

"This is great! Vickie will be happy if he can find somebody like you, and you'll be happy if you can find somebody like him. Then what are we waiting for?" joked Maya.

Megan just smiled.

Maya hugged Megan. "Welcome to our family, my child," she said.

At the same time Om and Natasha walked into the kitchen

Maya whispered, "Where is Vickie?"

Natasha did not know why her mother was whispering, but she whispered back, "I think he is taking a shower getting ready for the big celebration tonight."

"Good," she said.

Maya asked everybody to come near her, "Come here everybody and huddle. Whatever I am telling you, please, control your emotions. No screaming. I don't want Vickie to hear this."

Not knowing what was happening, Om and Natasha huddled. Megan knew what Maya was about to tell. She smiled.

"Again, no screaming" Maya warned again, "Vickie and Megan are going to get married."

Natasha was about to scream. Maya immediately put her hand on her mouth.

Maya continued, "OK guys, Here is the plan. Vickie has played several tricks on me. Now I want to play a trick on him and have the last laugh."

They looked at her curiously wondering what the plan was.

Maya continued, "Please don't let Vikram know anything about our plans. I am going to act like a typical Indian mother who is dreaming about finding a beautiful Indian wife for her son. I've never acted before, so please help me pull this one. So here is the plan."

CHAPTER XXXI

A Turning Point

The whole Srivastava family including Megan was sitting in the living room and drinking wine and munching on snacks. Maya finished her wine glass and asked Om for some more. Vikram was surprised to see his mother finish her wine so quickly.

He gave her thumbs up, "Way to go *Maa*."

Maya pretended to be a little more intoxicated than she actually was.

"Vickie, if an American citizen marries an Indian girl, how long does it take to get her the visa?" she asked acting to be drunk.

This question of Maya's caused a lot of worry for Vikram. "Why is she asking that?" he thought. "He is a US citizen. Is she asking this because she wants him to marry an Indian girl?" he wondered.

"Why do you ask that?" he asked.

"Just tell me that," she insisted.

Vikram tried to discourage her in thinking in the direction that he thought she was thinking. "These days it's is taking very long," he answered, "Sometimes even two years."

"Only two years! That is not too bad," she said acting unconcerned.

"But why are you asking that?" he asked worriedly.

She took another sip of wine. "Wait, I'm coming to that," she said.

At this point Vikram signaled to Om to ask him if he knew what was going on. But, unfortunately for Vikram, Om was also part of the act and he just shrugged his shoulders showing his ignorance. Natasha did the same. Vikram felt uncomfortable having this conversation in front of Megan.

Maya added a little more salt to his injury.

"I'm so happy that I found a perfect husband for Natasha. Now my only responsibility is to find a simple, homely Indian bride for Vikram," she revealed.

Vikram was very uncomfortable being in this situation, especially since Megan was there. He wondered what she must be thinking about all of this. He looked at Megan and signaled her to not worry. Being part of the act, Megan put on a confused look on her face showing her discomfort with the discussion.

At this point according to the plan Om decided to have some fun by pretending to help Vikram. He argued for Vikram. "But Vikram is living in a different country. He may want to find his own bride," he told Maya.

Vikram was curious to see how *Maa* would respond to this suggestion.

Maya called upon the actress from deep within her. She looked at Vikram and proudly said, "Are you kidding? Vikram is the best son any mother can ever have. Another tradition in Srivastava's family is that the children do not marry against their parents wishes."

Natasha put in her act by showing that she was on Vikram's side, "I did not know of this tradition, *Maa*."

Maya continued to add fuel to Vikram's frustration. "You need to trust your parents. They always know what is best for their children," she sermonized.

Vikram did not know how to react to this. Sometimes he looked at Megan trying to tell her that everything will be OK. Othertimes he looked at his father and sister asking for their help.

Then according to the plan, Maya winked at Megan signaling her to leave.

"I've to go to the bathroom," said Megan and left.

Vikram knew that Megan left because she did not like the way this conversation was going. But he felt helpless and again looked at Om and Natasha for help.

After Megan left, Maya continued, "*Beta* Vikram, I've lined up a really nice girl for you. I've called her in a restaurant tomorrow. We'll all go there and you can meet her, ask her anything you want."

Now Vikram was agitated and could not take it anymore. He snapped, "*Maa*, I don't want to see any girl. How can I marry somebody like that?"

Maya acted to be dumbfounded. "Are you saying you don't trust us? We will trap you with any girl?" she asked.

He did not know how to get out of this situation. "No *Maa*, I'm not saying that," he clarified.

Maya acted like a traditional Indian mother and made another appeal, "*Beta*, just see this girl once. She is a gem. When I saw her for the first time I fell in love with her. I'm confident you'll like her. But by any chance if you don't like her, I'll not insist on anything."

Then according to the next part of the plan Maya left to go to the bathroom and leave Vikram alone with Om and Natasha. "Hold that thought," she said while staggering to get up, "I've to go to bathroom. I'll be right back."

In the next part of the act, Om and Natasha were supposed to convice Vikram to agree to Maya's proposal of meeting this girl.

Vikram was really agitated. He wanted to scream, but he could not due to the fear that his mother would hear him. He whispered, "What is going on Pappa? Didn't you already talk to her about Megan?"

Om whispered back, "I tried to feel her out. I just asked her hypothetically about you and Megan and she started screaming. She didn't want to entertain that thought, even hypothetically. Looks like, she has already made up her mind about you."

Vikram pleaded to his father, "*Pappa* you know that I cannot not marry this girl. You'll have to help me get out of this."

Natasha jumped in, "I've a solution."

"What?" he said excitedly.

"What if you meet this girl and then say that you do not like her?" she proposed.

"Yes that is a great idea," Om concurred, "That way your mother will be satisfied that you saw the girl."

Vikram did not like this plan. "But that is not fair to this girl," he complained, "We are using her as a pawn."

"Do you have any other way out without upsetting *Maa*?" asked Natasha.

Vikram thought about it and decided reluctantly that this was the only way out.

"OK, I'll do that, but I don't want Megan to go through this drama or know anything about it," he cautioned.

Natasha and Om put on a blank face while laughing their heart out from within.

Vikram murmured to himself, "She'll probably think that I'm a coward. She'll not understand why I'm going to see the girl in the first place."

Vikram quickly conceived of his own plan to somehow keep Megan out of this drama. He looked at Natasha and said, "Natasha, I think you should tell *Maa* that Megan should not be told anything about this and should not be part of it."

Natasha stirred up his frustration a little more. "Why don't you tell Maa?" she asked.

"I can't," he chaffed, "Remember, Megan is your friend from your office. I've never met her before."

At that point, Maya walked in. Megan had not yet come back. Vikram knew why Megan did not return. She was probably upset.

Maya sat down. She asked Om to pour her another glass of wine. This was her third glass. Vikram had never seen Maya drink more than one glass of wine. After a few moments of silence, Vikram said, "*Maa*, I'll come tomorrow to meet this girl."

Maya pretended to be very joyful. "See? What did I tell you guys?" she said while looking at Om and Natasha, "I knew that my son will always listen to me." She got up and stumbled around to near Vikram. She hugged him and kissed him as if he was a little baby. He let her do that believing that she was quite drunk.

He signaled Natasha to tell *Maa* that Megan should not know about it.

"I suggest that Megan should not be told about it nor should be made part of this," suggested Natasha.

Maya acted surprised, "Why? Don't you want to show her our Indian traditions?"

"This is a dying Indian tradition *Maa*, and it makes a girl look like an object," said Natasha.

Vikram secretly gave Natasha thumbs up for her excellent reasoning. He didn't know that he was being double crossed.

Maya gave in to their demand, "OK, all you modern people I'm not going to argue about the traditions that people have been following from generations. If you insist, we can leave Megan out of this."

So *Maa*, when Megan is here, please don't talk about it," said Natasha showing that she was on Vikram's side, "And also we have to find some way to take care of her while we all go to meet this girl."

"Since she is from your work, can you ask Shweta to take her out for some sightseeing?" suggested Maya.

They all continued to weave a web around Vikram.

Vikram was now in no a mood to party anymore. He was still worried that Megan did not return. He asked Natasha to check on her. She went to her room. Megan was quietly sitting on a chair in her bedroom. Natasha peeped in to Megan's bedroom and gave her thumbs-up.

Megan whispered, "How is it going?"

"Everything is going according to the plan. Now it's time for you to make your face a little more blue and let's join them," instructed Natasha.

They walked to the party room. Vikran looked at Megan's face and tried to read her emotions. Megan did not make any eye contact with Vikram. He could clearly see depression on her face. But he felt helpless. He could not reveal anything to his mother right now because she was quite drunk. She might explode creating a very emabarassing situation. Although it was very uncomfortable situation for him, he knew that it'll all be over tomorrow when he met this girl and gave his verdict. After that he would explain to Megan everything and tell his mother about his relationship with Megan.

While Megan was there, nobody said a word about the girl that Vikram was trapped into meeting. After sitting there for a few minutes, Megan asked to be excused. "I think I had a bit too much to drink. If you don't mind I'll like to go to sleep," she said.

Maya acted surprised, "So soon, we have just started partying?"

"I feel sleepy. If you don't mind I'll like to go to bed," she insisted.

Vikram looked at Megan helplessly. He would have asked her to stay longer but he knew that it would be better if Megan left so she was not part of this senseless conversation.

Maya acted disappointed. "That is no problem," she said, "Have a good sleep. I'll see you in the morning."

Megan left. Vikram could not take this emotional torture any longer. He decided not to be part of this discussion. He also asked to be excused.

Om acted disappointed. "So that means the party is over?" he wondered.

"You guys can continue drinking," said Vikram while getting up to leave, "I need to be alone right now."

Maya pricked him a little more, "Take good rest. We have a very important day tomorrow. I'm going to drink some more. I'm very happy today. And I may be even happier tomorrow when Vikram meets and falls in love with this girl."

Vikram murmured, "I don't think so, *Maa*."

To show her support to her brother, Natasha also got up to leave.

Maya took another sip of wine. She was thoroughly enjoying her revenge on Vikram.

Now Maya and Om were alone in the room.

"Om, pour me another drink and pour one for you too. Lets talk some more," said Maya.

"Yes, it's too early to sleep," he replied.

Meanwhile, Vikram was restless in his room. He did not know how to make Megan feel better. He could not go to Megan's room because Maya and Om were sitting in the family room. He decided to call Natasha on her cellphone.

Natasha answered her phone.

"Sis, I feel strange with the whole situation," he told her.

She tried to make him relaxed, "*Bhaiyya*, I think you should relax. As *Pappa* said just go through the motion and you can always say that the girl is not your type."

"But it is utterly wrong and not fair to the girl," he protested.

"*Bhaiyya*, I don't think there is any other way out. If you go through this as Maa wants, it'll satisfy her and it'll also give us more time to work on her about Megan and you," she reasoned.

"I should not have agreed to this at all," he said, "I don't know what Megan must be going through. I don't know what to do."

"Don't worry about Megan," she advised, "I'll talk to her right now and explain the whole situation. Just go to sleep. We'll deal with this tomorrow."

CHAPTER XXXII

The Last Laugh

The next morning, while everybody else was enjoying the flawless execution of their plan, it was perhaps the worst day in Vikram's life. He was sitting quietly on breakfast table sipping tea with everybody. Megan sat away from him. She pretended to ignore him. She did not make eye contact with him. He was quite frustrated. He reasoned that as soon as this whole drama was over, he would be able to win her back.

According to the plan Natasha spoke, "Megan, Shweta called yesterday. She wanted to take you out for some sightseeing today. Do you want to go?"

Megan jumped at the offer, "Yes, sure. When is she coming?"

"She can be here in half-an-hour," she answered.

"Oh that will be great. I'll go and get ready," said Megan anxiously.

"I'll call her right now," said Natasha.

Natasha called Shweta to have her pick up Megan.

Vikram was relieved that Megan would not be part of this embarrassing drama. He had no clue that he was being set up by everybody.

Maya spoke in low voice pretending that Megan did not hear her, "We have to get ready too. We have to be there by 11 O'Clock. It's already 9:30. So let's go and get ready."

Vikram shook his head in disgust and slowly walked to his room to get ready.

While Vikram was getting ready, Shweta entered the house. Natasha handed over one package to Shweta. She left with Megan.

After some time Vikram came out wearing blue jeans and a white tee shirt. Maya looked at him and commented, "*Beta*, don't wear jeans and tee shirt, wear something nice, it may be a very important day of your life."

Vikram was already annoyed with his mother. "Yes, I know *Maa*. But I look fine," he said.

They all left to meet the mystry girl.

Maya, Om, Vikram and Natasha arrived at a restaurant. They were seated at a table in the middle of the restaurant. Maya looked at her watch and murmured, "I think they should be here in five minutes." In a couple minutes, her phone rang. Maya answered the phone, "Ok I'll be right out." She quickly put the phone away. She was visibly excited. "She is here. Natasha, let's go and get her," she announced. Vikram nervously looked on.

Maya quickly got up. "You sit here Vickie, she instructed, "Let's go Natasha."

Here on the table Vikram and Om sat alone. Vikram was very nervous. "*Pappa*, I'm not enjoying this moment at all," he told his father.

Om tried to psych him up, "As I told you, just go through the motions for the sake of your mother."

"But *Pappa*, first it's not fair to the girl. How will she feel when I tell her that I don't want to marry her? And secondly, it does not solve my problem. We have yet to tell *Maa* about Megan," said Vikram resentfully.

Om continued to egg him on, "Let's just go through that, and it'll buy us some more time. I'm sure we'll be able to come up with a plan."

At this moment Maya and Natasha slowly walked in with a sari draped mystry woman in their middle. Her head was partially covered in a veil.

Vikram glanced at her and murmured, "I don't believe I'm part of this. *Pappa*, who is she? Is she from 16th century? Why is she all covered up in veil?"

"Your mother told me that the girl is old fashioned but stunningly beautiful. Do you want me ask your mother to uncover her face?" he asked.

"No, No, Don't worry about it. I want this to be over as soon as possible," he replied.

As the veiled girl approached them, Om put his hand on Vikram's shoulder. "Calm down my son," he said, "You can do it."

Everybody in the restaurant looked at Maya and Natasha walking with a veiled girl dressed in sari.

Vikram again murmured to himself, "Oh God, please help me through this. It's so embarrassing."

Om got up from his chair to greet the girl. Vikram also stood up without looking at the girl. Om greeted the girl. The girl did not say anything. She just returned the greetings by a slight bend and folded hands. Her hands were covered with light colored stretch satin gloves. Om pulled a chair next to Vikram for the girl to sit. The girl continued to stand there.

"Let's leave. Give then some quiet time together," said Maya.

As soon as Vikram heard that they were leaving him alone with the girl, he got nervous. "You don't have to go," he told his mother.

She smiled at him and left with Om and Natasha.

Now Vikram and the girl were there alone, both standing.

"Please sit down," he said politely.

The girl did not say anything. She continued standing.

Vikram realized that she was perhaps waiting for him to sit first. He sat down. Then the girl sat down.

He paused, looked around, mustered some courage, and then spoke without even looking at her, "Listen, I don't want to lie to you. I am doing this just to please my mother. But the truth is that I am commited to somebody else. I am sure you are a wonderful girl, but I cannot marry you."

There was pin drop silence for a while. Then he could hear mild sobs coming from the veil. Vikram looked around to see if anybody was watching or hearing her sobs. He didn't know how to stop her from sobbing. "I know you must hate me for coming here and saying what I just said," he said, "I am really sorry. I should have never agreed to be part of this."

The girl's sobs became a little louder.

He again looked around for his parents for some help in this sticky situation.

"Please stop crying. Is there anything I can do to make you feel better?" he pleaded.

The girl shook her head in affirmative.

"I would like to feel just for once how it feels to be a bride," said the girl while still sobbing.

She continued, "Can you do me a favor just one time?"

He hesitated a little. "What is it?" he asked.

"Please uncover my veil with your hands and make me feel like a bride just for one moment," she appealed.

He was puzzled by this strange request. He argued, "But that will be all just an act."

The girl explained sobbingly, "I know, but I've never experienced that feeling and I don't know if I ever will. I'll spend the rest of my life re-living this moment again and again."

"This girl is not only old fashioned, she is a little crazy too," he wondered. But since there was no way to get out of this situation without doing what she wanted, he mustered enough courage to lift the girl's veil. He started to lift her veil while turning his head sideways, closing his eyes and not looking at her face. The girl's face was now totally uncovered.

Out came the beautiful face of Megan, dressed up like an Indian bride. She smiled and gently put her hands on top of his hands. He twitched his eyes tightly believing that this strange girl was holding his hand. He tried to pull his hand away but she did not let go. He felt helpless. He slowly opened his eyes and turned his head toward her. As soon as he saw the face of Megan behind the veil, he almost choked. He did not know how to react. At the same time Maya, Om and Natasha walked in laughing and clapping. He laughed with joy too but it was a laugh showing the feeling of relief, being defeated in his own game, and being double crossed by everybody.

"Son, this was the taste of your own medicine," said Maya.

He was at a loss for words.

Natasha chimed in, "So *Bhaiyya*, what is the verdict? Was *Maa* right when she said that you'll fall in love with the girl as soon as you saw her?"

"Sis, remember that your parents are never wrong," he said.

Now since all the suspense was out, Om called for another celebration. He spoke in a king like voice, "Son, do you remember how Srivastavas celebrate their great moments?"

"Yes Your Highness! It has been the tradition of Srivastava family to celebrate our happy occasions by consuming a large amount of alcohol."

Om continued to speak in a king like voice, "That is right my son. You should always remember and follow your family traditions."

Vikram added, "And what a coincidence *Pappa*, Megan told me that her family has exactly the same tradition."

Om again spoke in a king like voice, "Remember son, great minds think alike, and I hope that you two will continue the tradition for many years to come…"

"But I want to put a stop to one tradition," Maya jumped in.

"Which tradition?" asked Om while the rest looked on curiously.

"In the last two weeks, you all have taught me a very important lesson. I feel that I am a changed person," said Maya, "So, here on this important occasion, I make a solemn pledge to you all."

"There are many people in this world who have the ability to value an individual based only on his or her qualities, not their skin color," she continued, "I want to be one of those people. My pledge to you is that all the nonsensical rituals that I followed until now will have no place in my life any more."

While Natasha and Vikram were not sure, Om knew deep down in his heart that Maya meant every word she spoke. It appeared to be a turning point in Maya's life.

CHAPTER XXXIII

No Black Tea Please

A year had passed by. Vikram was married to Megan and living happily with her in the US. Natasha was married to Ashok and living happily in another town.

Natasha was in her home and did not feel well. She went to bathroom. She felt like throwing up. After she came out of the bathroom, she called Ashok.

He came running. "What is wrong?" he asked.

"I feel queasy. Perhaps I ate something bad yesterday," she said.

"Let me call my friend, Dr. Sinha. Perhaps she can stop by on her way to the hospital and examine you," he said.

He called his friend, and then returned to Natasha.

Meanwhile she rested on her bed while Ashok rubbed her hands to make her feel better.

After some time the doorbell rang.

He ran to the door and greeted Dr. Sinha. He escorted her to Natasha's room.

Dr. Sinha examined her. She had a very serious look on her face. Ashok looked at her and got concerned. Dr. Sinha gave her verdict, "My dear friend, you have a very serious problem. There seems to be some new growth in her stomach."

Ashok and Natasha were both shocked to hear that. They looked at the doctor for answers.

Dr. Sinha continued, “I don’t know what you did to her, but whatever you did, that has triggered all kinds of reactions into her stomach. And these reactions will continue for 9 months.”

“Dr. Sinha, are you saying what I think you’re saying?” he screamed.

“Yes, I’m saying what I think you think I’m saying,” answered Dr. Sinha, “Congratulations! You are going to be parents.”

Ashok closed his eyes and could hardly contain his excitement.

“Please call me in the next couple of days. Right now everything is normal,” said the doctor as she left.

Ashok returned to Natasha, held her hands and they were both very happy.

After a few minutes she asked him, “I’m a little thirsty. Can you get me something to drink?”

“Yes Maam, I’ll be right back,” he said.

He went to kitchen and decided to get her favorite drink, the black tea. He prepared the black tea and brought it to her.

She took the cup of black tea, but before she could take the first sip, she paused and rememberd all what her mother used to do and say about the effects of black tea. She put the cup down without taking a sip.

“What happened? Is the black tea not good?” he asked.

“No, it’s not that. I won’t drink black tea. Please get me some milk,” she said.

“That is a great idea. The child will probably need milk,” he concurred.

“And, can you do me another favor?” she asked again.

“I’m always at your service Maam,” he said smilingly.

“Please go and buy me some fresh coconuts and cashews. And then scrape the dark skin off the coconut white,” she instructed, “Until the baby is born, I’ll eat the coconut white only.”

“Are these your family’s recipes for a healthy and beautiful child?” he asked.

“Yes,” she said.

She did not want to give him the details on the effect of coconut and other stuff that her mother used to believe and practice to ensure that the child would have lighter skin. During her past conversations with him, she always argued against this aspect of her mother’s behavior. If he found out that she was practicing exactly the same meaningless rituals her mother used to, he would think that she was a hypocrit.

He teased her, “Clearly, they must work. Because see how beautiful you are.”

She smiled. "Please come back quickly from work. We'll call our parents after you're back," she told him.

"I'll be back in a jiffy," he said, "But what about you? Are you not going to work?

"No, I'll work from home today," she said.

She rested on the bed fantacising about her unborn child. Simultaneously she was re-living in her mind all those rituals that her mother used to do to ensure a light skin colored child. One of them was to avoid looking at any dark skinned person first thing in the morning. She was struggling in her mind about the baselessness of those beliefs but it was the future of her unborn child. "What if there is any truth to those beliefs? Should she take any chance? Does she want a dark skinned child? Does she want her child to go thorugh the humiliations that she endured?" she struggled with these questions." "It was a matter of only nine months," she wondered, "If the child is dark skinned girl, she will face the same difficulties that her *Maa* and she experienced." She always questioned her mother about the frivolity of the rituals that her mother used to follow. "No, she was not going to perpetuate these meaningless things," she told herself. But, one question kept popping in her head - What if there was any truth to those beliefs?

Ashok came back from work in the evening. "I'm back. I'll grate the coconut white and bring it to you. What do you want me do with cashews?" he asked.

"Bring them as is," she instructed.

He grated the coconut white and brought it with a glass of milk and cashews. "Here you go," he said, "Let's call our parents.Whom do you want to call first?"

"Let's call your parents first," she suggested.

He called his parents. While the phone was ringing, he asked her if she wanted to be the one to tell the big news.

"No you do it," she said.

His mother answered the phone.

"Hey Mom, we have great news. You're going to be a *Dadi Maa*," he blurted it out.

"Oh really, that is wonderful news," said Mrs. Mathur happily, "When did you find out?"

"Today," he said.

"Let me talk to Natasha," she said.

Ashok handed over the phone to Natasha.

Ashok's mother gave her the instructions about pregnancy, "*Betey*, I am so happy to hear this. This is your first child. You have to take all kinds of precautions. Don't forget that now you have to eat for two people."

"Yes," she said.

"I would have come and lived with you to help you through this pregnancy but I cannot leave Mr. Mathur due to his medical situation," said Mrs. Mathur, "I think you should have your mother come and help you."

"Yes, I'll call my *Maa*," she said.

"Mrs. Srivastava will be so happy to hear this news," said Mrs. Mathur.

They chatted for some more time. Mrs. Mathur gave her several tips on healthy pregnancy.

After they finished talking, they called Natasha's parents. This time he proposed that Natasha should break the news to her parents.

"Hi *Maa*, I've good news to tell you," said Natasha excitedly, "You're going to be a *Nani Maa*."

Maya was ecstatic to hear this.

She immediately called out for Om, "Om, come here quick. You are going to be a *Nana*."

Om ran to near the phone.

"When did you find that out?" Maya asked.

"Today," she said.

Maya could not contain her excitement, "Oh that is great news."

Like any typical mother the first thing that came to her mind was that her daughter will need help since it was her first child. "Listen, this is your first pregnancy. You need to be careful. I've a lot of vacation days left in my job. I can easily take two months off to come there towards the end of your pregnancy and help you," she told her.

While she was talking to her mother, she was reliving in her mind what her mother used to preach. She had told her that she would not see her maid servant's face in the morning because the maid servant was dark skinned. Her *Maa* was also dark skinned. "*Maa* would be deeply hurt if she discovered that I did not take her help because of her dark skin," she feared, "But if my mother's teachings were true, I may be risking giving birth to a dark skinned child." Natasha was struggling with these conflicting thoughts in her mind while her *Maa* continued to talk on phone.

"Natasha, are you there?" wondered Maya.

Natasha was startled as if she just woke up. "Yes, I'm here. *Maa*, don't make any plans for coming here yet," said Natasha hurriedely, "Let me call you about it."

"Did you tell Mrs. Mathur about it?" asked Maya.

"Yes, we just told her," she replied.

"And Vickie?" asked Maya again.

"Not yet, I'm going to call him right now," she said.

They talked for a while mostly about healthy eating during her pregnancy.

* * *

Several months had passed. It was about two months before Natasha's delivery. She needed help to go through her pregnancy. She knew that Ashok was not keen on hiring a maid primarily due to two reasons – 1) they were relatively new to the town and did not have many friends to help them find a trusted maid, and 2) there had been several burgalaries in their neighborhood in which several maids were found to be involved. The only person that could help her was her mother. But...what about the potential risks to her unborn child's skin color? She continued to fight her internal struggle. Finally, the selfish mother in her won - she decided that she was not going to risk her child's appearance by the presence of her dark skinned mother. She conceived of a plan to mislead Ashok, her mother, and her mother-in-law. All she could think at that point was her unborn child. She did not worry about any other consequences. She was so blinded by her motherly instincts that it did not occur to her that sooner or later the truth will be revealed. She tricked Ashok into believing that her mother couldn't come due to her busy work. She lied to her mother-in-law, and told her that her mother would come and help her. The touchiest task was to trick her own mother. She called her mother and told her that Ashok's mother was going to come and help her through the pregnancy.

"Oh, that is very nice of her," said Maya, "But if Mrs. Mathur has any problems, do let me know. And drink a lot of milk, eat coconut white and cashews, and definitely no black tea! Please do everything that I told you to do."

"Yes *Maa*, that is exactly what I'm doing," said Natasha while grimacing.

Natasha was hoping and praying that her plan would not leak, at least until her delivery, so there was no risk to the skin color of her unborn child. Like a mother on a mission, she followed all the precaution and the rituals that her mother used to.

Natasha and Ashok managed to go through the pregnancy on their own. She played both Mrs. Mathur and Maya into believing that the other one was there helping her.

* * *

It was the delivery day. Natasha was in the hospital.

She had just delivered a baby girl. It was like the history repeating itself. Like her mother, the first thing in Natasha's mind was her daughter's skin color. As soon as the nurse handed her the baby and she saw the baby's fair cheeks, she was euphoric. She forgot all her pains. She wanted to see more of her to make sure that she was not dreaming. She quickly uncovered baby's feet and arms. She moved baby's arms and legs sideways to make sure that she was fair everywhere - "Yes!!" my daughter is *gori*." She felt as if she conquered the world. She was so proud of herself. "Everything that I did must have worked," she thought.

"Can I also see my daughter?" Ashok interrupted.

As if woken up from a beautiful dream, Natasha was startled. She looked up.

"Ashok, look how fair she is," she was almost choking with happiness.

She knew that her daughter could drink black tea, black coffee, or whatever else she wanted. She knew that her daughter would not have to wear long pants and full sleeve shirts to hide her skin. She knew that her daughter would not need any skin painting treatment. She knew that her daughter would not have to put skin whitening cream on every night. She knew that when her daughter grew up, boys would line up to marry her. She knew that the most wonderful future awaited her daughter. She wanted the whole world to know about her most fair and beautiful girl.

"Ashok, please call everybody and tell them the good news," she said.

Ashok walked out of the delivery room and called his mother first, "Mom, Natasha just delivered a beautiful healthy daughter."

"Oh that is wonderful news. How are Natasha and the baby?" she asked.

While he was talking to his mother, he noticed his cellphone battery dying. "Yes Mom, everybody is doing fine. My cellphone battery is dying, can you call Natasha's mother and tell her this news," said Ashok.

His mother was always under the impression that Maya was there helping Natasha.

"Why? Is Mrs. Srivastava not there?" she asked.

Before he could answer her, his cellphone went dead.

Mrs. Mathur was a little perplexed. Her husband was standing right beside her.

"I thought that Mrs. Srivastava was helping Natasha during her pregnancy," she mumbled.

"May be she was. She may have just left her there for a few days," reasoned Mr. Mathur.

Mrs. Mathur immediately called Maya.

Maya checked her phone. It was Mrs. Mathur calling. Maya got really excited. She was under the impression that Mrs. Mathur was with Natasha and that she must have called to give Natasha's delivery news. "Ommm," she called out, "it is Mrs. Mathur calling. Come quickly."

Om came running. He wanted to hear what Mrs. Mathur had to say. "Put your phone on speaker," he told her.

She put the phone on speaker and answerd the phone.

"Mrs. Srivastava, Congratulations!! You just became a *Nani Maa*," announced Mrs. Mathur, "Natasha delivered a baby girl."

Maya was happy to hear the news. She was anxious to know more about her grand daughter. "Oh that is wonderful news. How does the baby look?" she asked.

"I don't know," said Mrs. Mathur, "They have not sent me her pictures yet."

Maya was confused. "Her pictures…? Are you not there with them?" she asked.

Mrs. Mathur did not know what was going on. "No, I could not go there because of Mr. Mathur's medical situation," she revealed, "Natasha had told me that you were there helping her."

All of a sudden, Maya was dumbfounded.

Maya stood there dazed as if she was struck by lightening. She turned toward Om with a bewildered look on her face. "Why did she do such a thing? Why did she not let me help her? Why did she lie to me?" she muttered.

Om took a deep breath, "Like a good daughter, she did exactly what she learnt from you."

*********************** THE END ************************

Glossary

Angrezi babu: Pronounced as ung-ray-zee baa-boo; an English speaking white European male

Angrezi mem: Pronounced as ung-ray-zee may-m'; an English speaking white European female

Arey: pronounced as written; It has similar meaning as "Oh" in English.

Ashram: pronounced as aa-sh-r-m; A secluded place where a community can live in peace and tranquility amidst the nature.

Auto rikshaw: In addition to regular taxis and city buses, auto rikshaws are common mode of transportation-for-hire in India. These are three-wheelers having seating for four in the back. The driver sits in front.

Babu: pronounced as b-aa-b-oo; an affectionate way of addressing a young boy.

Beta: pronounced as bey-taa; An affectionate way of addressing you son. Sometimes, the other elders will also affectionately refer to males much younger than them as *beta*.

Beti: pronounced as bey-tee; An affectionate way of addressing you daughter. Sometimes, the other elders will also affectionately refer to females much younger than them as *beti*.

Betey: pronounced as bey-tey; An affectionate way of addressing either a son or a daughter.

Bhabhi: pronounced as bhaa-bhee; Brothers or sisters refer to their elder brother's wife as *bhabhi*. In Indian culture, it's unrespectful to address your elders by their names. Thus addressing elder brother's wife as *bhabhi* is showing your respect to her. It's also a common practice to address your friend's wife as *bhabhi*. This shows that you consider your friend as your brother.

Bhaiyaa: pronounced as bh-ai-y-aa; big brother

Chaat: pronounced as written; it's a generic name of a variety of spicy snacks.

Chacha: pronounced as chaa-chaa; uncle (father's younger brother)

Chachi: pronounced as chaa-chee; aunt (father's younger brother's wife)

Cheese Pakora: Pronounced as cheez p-koraa; deep fried cheese pieces wrapped with mixture of flour and spices.

Chotey Babu: pronounced as ch-oa-tey b-aa-b-oo; little boy

Chotey Sarkar: pronounced as ch-oa-tey sar-kaar; *chotey* means little, *sarkar* means master. *Chotey Sarkar* means little master

Dholak: pronounced as dho-l'-k; a two sided drum played fingers of both hands

Dadi Maa: pronounced as d-aa-d-ee m-aa; paternal grand mother

Gora: pronounced as goa-raa; A term used to describe a very light skin colored male

Gori: pronounced as goa-ree; A term used to describe a very light skin colored lady

Gudiya: pronounced as gu-di-yaa; a pretty doll

Habshi: pronounced as h'-b'-shee: black Africans

Halwa: pronounced as h-l-waa; a sweet paste similar to grits.

Inquelab Zindabad: pronounced as in-k'-laab zinda-baad; means long live our nation. The Indian freedom fighters while fighting the British Empire used to shout these as slogan to pump up patriotic feelings in people.

Jalebi: pronounced as ja-ley-bee; a pretzel shaped crispy fried dough filled with sugar syrup.

Ji: pronounced as j-ee; this is normally added after the names to show respect.

Katori: pronounced as ka-tow-ree; a small metal bowl used for serving small quantities of food.

Kaala: pronounced as kaa-laa; A derogatory term used to describe a very dark skinned male

Kaali: pronounced as kaa-lee; A derogatory term used to describe a very dark skinned lady

Kaali billi: pronounced as kaa-lee billee; A black cat. Sighting a *kaali billi* is considered to be a bad omen especially if a *kaali billi* crosses you path. Some Indians believe that if a kaali billi crosses your path and if you continue walking, bad things will happen to you.

Kaali ghata: pronounced as kaa-lee ghataa; Describes the very dark clouds that you see before an impending rain or thunderstorm.

Kaali Maa: pronounced as k-aa-l-ee m-aa; *Kaali* means black, and *Maa* means mother. Thus, *Kaali Maa* is another incarnation of Indian God depicted as a black woumen with many supernatural powers primarily to punish wrong doers.

Kabab: pronounced as k-baab; Spicy snack made with ground meat.

Kajal: pronounced as kaa-j'-l'; the black mascara that girls use to highlight their eyes.

Kurta-paijama: pronounced as ku'-rt-aa pai-j-aa-m-aa; a casual and comfortable clothing usually worn by men. Kurta is the knee length loose shirt. The *paijama* is a loose fitting pajama.

Maa: pronounced as written; mother

Maalik: pronounced as written; *Maalik* means a master or owner. In strict sense *Maalik* refers to God. But often times the household servants use this word to refer to their male bosses.

Masala dosa: pronounced as ma-sa-laa dough-saw; A popular South Indian dish (it's popular throughout India) that is spicy potato concoction wrapped in a thin (almost paper thin) fried tortilla made from rice flower.

Mem Sahib: pronounced as maim-saahib; *Mem* is used for a white woman and *Sahib* means superior. During the Britsh rule in India, the Indian servants working in British families used to address their white female bosses as *Mem Sahib*. Now 60 years after British have left India, the tradition still continues except that now the address their Indial female bosses as *Mem Sahib*.

Namastey promounced as n-m-s-tay; and Indian greeting

Nana pronounced as n-aa-n-aa; maternal grand father.

Nani Maa pronounced as n-aa-n-ee m-aa; maternal grand mother

Pakori: pronounced as p'-ko-ree; deep fried, bite-sized, ball shaped concoction of chopped onions, dough, peppers and spices.

Pappa pronounced as written; same as papa, dad or father

Pooja: pronounced as poo-jaa; a prayer to God.

Roti: pronounced as roa-tee; puffed bread

Saanvla: pronounced as saa-n'-vlaa; A term used to describe a male having skin shade in between light and dark. This term can be insulting to boys depending on how and when it's used. For example, if you use word *saanvla* to describe a man whose skin color is closer to the lighter side, he may not like it. He would prefer to be called *gora*. Whereas, if you use *saanvla* to refer to a male whose skin color is closer to the dark side, he will be pleased. To refer to a *saanvla* male as *kaala* will not be appreciated. Generally, girls are more sensitive to this than boys.

Saanvli: pronounced as saa-n'-vlee; A term used to describe a female having skin shade in between light and dark. This term can be insulting to girls depending on how and when it's used. For example, if you use the word *saanvli* to describe a woman whose skin color is closer to the lighter side, she may not like it. She would prefer to be called *gori*. Whereas, if you use *saanvli* to refer to a female whose skin color is closer to the dark side, she'll be pleased. To refer to a *saanvli* girl as *kaali* will not be appreciated. Generally, girls are more sensitive to this issue than boys.

Salwar kurta: pronounced as spelled; popular attire wore by Indian females.

Samosa: pronounced as s-moa-saa; A popular Indian snack – a prism-shaped crushed spicy potato wrapped in a fried crispy dough shell.

Sari: pronounced saa-ree; it's 4 to 9 meters long strip of unstiched cloth that Indian female drape over their body in various styles. It's common female garment for Indian women.

Sasuraal: pronounced as s'-su-raal; in-law's house

Printed in the United States
209747BV00001B/107/P

9 780595 530182